WITH TEETH

Dear Will —

I'm so grateful for the time +
opportunity I had to spend with
you + with your writing. Please
keep creating + making smart,
funny, & weird + heart-felt things.

Best to you + yours +
don't be a stranger —

WITH TEETH,
NATANYA ANN PULLEY

MVP Winner #140

New Rivers Press 50th Anniversary 1968-2018

©2019 by Natanya Ann Pulley

First Edition

Library of Congress Control Number: 2018962076

ISBN: 978-0-89823-389-6

e-ISBN: 978-0-89823-390-2

New Rivers Press is a nonprofit literary press associated with Minnesota State University Moorhead.

Cover and interior design by Kelsey Curfman

Cover art by Zandria Ann Sturgill

Cover art photo by Nick Higer

Author photo by Gray Warrior

The publication of *WITH TEETH* is made possible by the generous support of Minnesota State University Moorhead, the Dawson Family Endowment, and oth er contributors to New Rivers Press.

NRP Staff: Nayt Rundquist, Managing Editor; Kevin Carollo, Editor; Travis Dolence, Director
Trista Conzemius, Art Director

Interns: Alyssa Berry, Olivia Carlson, Sarah Ernster, Alex Ferguson, Laura Grimm, Aubrey Johnson, Lauren Phillips

WITH TEETH book team: Evonne Eichhorn, Allison Funk, Logan Peterson, Zepherian Richardson, Maddie Schmidt

(∞) Printed in the USA on acid-free, archival-grade paper.

WITH TEETH is distributed nationally by Small Press Distribution.

 New Rivers Press
c/o MSUM
1104 7th Ave S
Moorhead, MN 56563
www.newriverspress.com

for shideezhí

Fierce, harrowing, haunting, holy, Natanya Ann Pulley's exhilarating fictions are lit by love and throbbing with sorrow. Thomas Merton says, "The human body is a body of broken bones." Inventing playful, subversively poignant ways to tell our most devastating stories saves us from the isolation of grief and restores us to the consolations of community. The turbulent tales of With Teeth rupture despair with delight, delivering the reader to a dizzy delirium of pleasures, sweet surprise, mercy, and the redemptive alchemy of laughter. Words, the right words—the magical, transformative spells we cast through webs of language—help us navigate our endless maze of bewilderments: we need not suffer alone: others have endured and survived unfathomable losses—multitudes known and unknown have not been crushed or destroyed by disease, betrayal, the deaths and disappearances of those most loved, the swells and surges of their own terrifying impulses. Affliction makes us human and humane, compassionate and humble. Those unafraid to witness, those who hunger to be pierced with tenderness, those who mourn will find refuge in these radiant stories, solace and hope, deep joy and the infinite bliss of surrender. As one speaker so lovingly says: "It's the end of the world and you feel fine and which ice cream do you want?" Yes, it is the end of the world; we are near the end of our lives, and even now lovers kiss: "16 years of this, he and I. . . . Don't move away. Let it start here, now, I tell myself. . . . The large 'O' of my mouth forms. Hold it. Don't let it go." Even now, "if this pathetic old pastor and this weird heart-girl are going to exchange anything tonight, it better start with a safeword." Yes, my darling, angry, runaway girl, I let you go, it's the end of the world, and even now "If the DNA of us every time added up in the same way. . . . If there were the slightest chance we could make you again, I think your father wouldn't hesitate."
—Melanie Rae Thon, author of *Voice of the River*, *Silence & Song*, and *The 7th Man*

CONTENTS

A PROLOGUE WITH TEETH

She wears a mask that looks like her. It slopes severely at the nose with cheeks set far back below the cheekbones. The sides of her face: the color of a split pear. Grainy when on the lips. Through her mask she says "ah" when a stranger tells her he is shedding his most recent sun-burn. She asks what he is becoming. The sound from her lips barely catches on the mask's lips. She once imagined the tails and ears of her words never making it through her masklips and falling between the skins, digging trenches. That if ever the mask were removed her warts and cracks would show. But years of practice changed everything. She rarely wishes someone could see her for what she really is. In fact, she often forgets it is there. As does everyone else.

To a clerk she shows pictures of fish with teeth. *With Teeth*, she says and reveals her own. The crowns. The fillings. The un-coloring from a baking soda and peroxide paste unable to reach the curved spaces between. That yellowed surface before it ducks behind a slightly inflamed red gum. Her teeth, a memory of teeth. Her mouth, teeth-worn.

He shakes his head. She flips a page, her mouth still open. Another fish, this one with human-looking teeth. *With Human Teeth*, she says and slams it on the counter. *Fish With Teeth. Gar fish . . . alligator gar fish, snakehead fish and, of course, the piranha. Razors. Shark-like. Shark-fish-like.*

Shark-fish-like, the clerk repeats.

Sheepshead fish, she says. *With human(like) Teeth.* Those incisors. Smooth and solid. Pluckable. Denture-able teeth. *Teeth that could bring that fish out of the water to a plate of pasta. No minnows, algae, river scum, or salmon eggs. No no no.* She crumples up her cash before handing it over. *Combo meals! Vending machine snacks! The kind of teeth that would take a fish to a couch, belly-up*, she says.

He says he hasn't seen any. He sells her duct tape, sanding paper, and wallpaper that looks like stained wood. She asks him to ask around.

The sheepshead fish, she says when the glass door of her shop won't budge. Jingle of keys. Her slight weight pushed against the glass. Wait for the bells on the other side to say, *We are in.*

The sheepshead fish was a man. The front door of her pawn and curio shop scoots open. The distinct smell of too many old things at once pulls her in. The door no longer her obstacle, she finds herself back behind the counter—purse, shopping bag, and keys placed away. Away away. She yawns, stretches, and then pulls herself back into herself.

The sheepshead fish was ONCE a man, she says aloud to no one in her shop. Readied and assured, those words hang lower on the lip, falling along the crest of her mask. The sheepshead fish was once a bold man. A man that talked a lot around town. He said things no one would say. He told people what time it was exactly. He knew the longitude and latitude of many great (and not-so-great) places. He was a man who knew things and said so; he had no face beneath his face.

Or he was a rude man. He listened to gossip and repeated it loudly. He said the things that typically slide along the sidewalks and backrooms of a town. He said them with a smile and no regret. He was all mask-face. Masks on masks. And a witch heard him once and turned him into a fish. With Teeth.

Or he was always a fish, she says. She puts her hands up to her outer face and taps on her nose. No one sees this. But she knows this story is almost true. A fish that swallowed a man. But a man that knew too much and kept all his knowing in his teeth. The teeth stayed; the man did not.

Or . . . it was a woman.

A woman that plucked the teeth from her lover. A remembrance. A hope. She took them while he slept. He had said so many words. He had said *all* the words. All the words that mattered. She had once looked up along the cracks in the ceiling thinking of all the words that would matter to be said. And realized he had said them. And there were no words left. No words to be said to her. Only those actions. Those steals of looks and tiny grins . . . at first. And then those other actions, the ones that took those words apart. He might work late. He might not like the way she reorganized his records. He might learn to repeat those words while resenting her for always being there in his bed, when those other ladies, the ones that don't need the words, were standing outside his door. So she took those teeth. And more than likely, after realizing a jar might turn them stale, she ate them. Thinking she could keep them inside. And not being a witch or a type of forest magic or a very bright girl, she did not grind up the teeth or use any sort of oils, which might help her body absorb the teeth into her blood and straight to her heart. Instead, the teeth sat in her stomach for two days as she worried. Worried he would notice and leave her. Which he did.

She was then a sad girl. A distraught girl. A girl with words of a lover in her gut. She was not bright enough to imagine them gnawing at her. She just imagined them there in her gut smiling and speaking those words again and again.

Like all sad and distraught and not-so-bright girls, she ran to the river to talk to a fish. A fish that had no knowledge of men or women and the heartbreak and troubles they occupied themselves with, but a fish that would speak as if it did. It was the sheepshead fish and was more than likely annoyed to be related (in name) to a sheep because it had never seen one. And like all fish in rivers talking to people, it tricked her. It might have said as much as, "If you come in the river, I will swim into your stomach and take out the teeth," which is exactly what it did.

And for a moment when the girl's mouth was as wide as it possibly could be, when the unmasked skin around her chin began to reach up to her wide cheekbones, hoping to pull itself back up, when her tongue began to wonder the taste of chewed fish scales, when that great fish plunged (sheep's)head first into her gaping maw . . . she was no longer a not-so-bright girl and she realized something the forest nymphs and witches of her little world might understand that she too now had suspicion of. She gathered from the week's experiences that this sort of situation was one to be avoided.

Of course, the fish entered her stomach. Grabbed the teeth. And ate its way out.

And she, a pulpy mess of once-her-body, drifted throughout the river, to feed the river animals and fish. A smorgasbord. Although our storyteller wasn't Swedish, it was the first word that came to the woman's mind.

Satisfied by her retelling of the origin of the sheepshead fish, the woman practiced it several times. First muttering those words and letting some tumble about on her own tongue and onto her lips (masked or not), often wondering the taste of fish scales as well as what it might be like to have a man's teeth that could eat human food.

She had nothing to tidy in the shop. Nothing new but the wall and sandpaper and duct tape, which she wasn't moved to use just yet. She had no messages, no mail. No books to tend. No messes to sort this day, a Tuesday, which she believed was never the day for too much sorting. And she had only to practice the story before she could swim through the telling of it to no one in particular—except perhaps to a few imaginary people that might listen. One was a tall man, who often wore collared knit shirts, always plain knit shirts: red, blue, and sometimes a tan-colored one. And he would come by her store hoping to find a good deal on something that one finds out they need only too late, too late to actually afford a new one or a decently-priced used one online. He had no friends from whom to borrow. Perhaps he had no friends. And he needed something like a chainsaw or a lawn mower. Her other imagined listener was (as most of the people in her shop are) looking for money, bringing in appliances and tools and silver candlesticks (how they all still had weighty candlesticks!) from their homes. These visitors, looking for cash (the kind that smelled used) and always walking by and ignoring the wall displays:

An El Chupacabra in its glass case. Shriveled skin, the color of old wine.

The broadside torn along the bottom right corner. Titled *Fantastic Freaks*. Its captives' bulbous and triple limbs and lack of limbs always well lit.

Perhaps they would turn for a moment to (or instinctually away from) the silent wax people, but always they would move to the counter, glance at guns, and then sell their mother's wedding ring.

The final pair of imagined listeners was by far her favorite and as she talked to the imaginary them, she would work up a voice loud enough to fool any mask intent on keeping the words slurred or smothered. The listeners only came in now and again: us tourists. Stumbling through the small town waiting for some other event, we would notice outside the pawnshop a worn and dusty wood panel: "Curious Oddities Inside. See a wax Hitler, Today only! Monsters from every corner of the world! And the first and complete collection of Fish With Teeth!" We, wasting time before dinner or a festival or meeting strangers which we had planned to meet—we, traveling twins and drift of half-awake selves open to a world behind the world as only tourists with time to kill (and children and the delightfully delusional) often are, would enter slowly and veer to the south wall. The marvelous, the bizarre, the mangled and glossy bodies and animals . . . another type of smorgasbord to be feasted on by us river folk. Eating up pieces of the dull doomed girls of the world, letting skins and bones catch on our teeth. And one of us, usually a polite or shy or polite-and-shy girl (because the men were always looking at the shrunken heads), would ask about the sheepshead fish and if (don't tell!) it could be real.

The woman would walk over from behind her counter and clear her throat a little and tell the story of the fish that reached down the throat of the not-so-bright young lover, and the woman would tell the story as if she had heard it from whatever soul brought in the fish to the pawn shop, but also as if she had heard it from long before, as if she was born with this story and only upon seeing the great fish for the first time did the words come to being. The woman would tell the story and her mask, this mask that looked like her would become a little brittle—in danger of flaking off, exposing those incisors and molars and, oh yes, why not, maybe even human-fish carnassials this time. *Her face flaking almost like scales*, we'll say when retelling the story to our somewhat friends and acting-amused acquaintances back home. We'll say it began with a fish—no, With Teeth. Every story begins With Teeth.

NATANYA ANN PULLEY

CANNIBAL

He said it was to absorb my power. The way they talk about cannibals in the movies. He said it was because he had a hole inside him that he stuffed and stuffed but could never fill. I told him we all have holes and he said he knew it and it didn't matter what I thought as he started with a toe, which I thought was unwise. So little meat in the fingers and toes. Start with the shoulder.

Still, there I was inside him and I could hear his grumbling, then the weeping, and I worried I'd find someone else in there with me.

But I must have been the first. There was more than a hole. There was an expanse. An expanse in him, miles wide. Miles deep. Miles high, more than that because there are more than three dimensions inside each of us. It was miles back in time and miles into dreams. Miles and miles of him and no hole to find.

At first, I kept quiet. I worried I'd wake him at night or disrupt him in a meeting, while ordering coffee, or when he'd fall into a reverie doing the dishes. The water, the scrubbing, the thought of cleanliness. Pruned fingers. Smell of sunflower soaps.

Eventually there were too many miles, too much of him. And when I got tripped up in his ligaments to get a better ear on a conversation he had with some detectives who came by, I heard myself catch his breath. I don't know if he heard it too, but it began a long line of me trying out hums and breaths and coughs and guttural rhythms. I didn't want to spook him with my words and I was never sure I could.

I don't know what power I brought to him, if any. I don't know of anything called strength in the two of us. But I do know that I could howl and it kept him up at night. I could scream and he could try to shake or run me out. Sometimes he'd run and I'd say words. Nothing of sense or sentences or significance. I'd say some words in any order and he'd try to run them out.

If you were to have asked me before if a person could live inside another, I would have said yes. I would have said that many of the men I've known have lived in me. I took them with me wherever I went. I would have said that mothers and celebrities live and die in us. I would have said nice things about childhood too.

But I wouldn't have said that I walked miles in another person or that I found nothing and he found nothing and instead we were a walking, breathing nothing. We are not solid things with a hole to fill, hole edges to maintain, and sod and grit hauled from other parts of ourselves into this chasm. No, we are an emptiness and when we feel a hole, it is only because we came across something solid for a brief moment and thought we were solid too. The lies he told himself about what is solid. The delusions he had of ground.

I remember when I too lived in a skin of my own and thought myself whole.

So it mattered little when he confessed. When the police shuffled about looking so less than the thinking and flawed machines on TV crime shows. When there was time time time as he waited for paperwork to sign. Even some somethings later in a courtroom with my father and sister near, it mattered little. They nodded and sobbed and held one another. Holding onto each other's nothingness in hopes that what was made solid by their arms stayed within them. My children in another room somewhere, another life somewhere. And my husband a crush of himself, so much smaller than I remembered. My consumer saw them too.

I knew he wouldn't be able to live with me here, wondering what was to become of us. I thought this so often and imagined the possibilities of us as not us that when he tightened a sheet or rope around his neck, I was pretty sure he wanted to know too. When he swallowed me, when he thought me a strong spirit to ingest, he didn't know how little I was. He didn't know we'd grow exponentially into nothing. But I must have known. The way I always knew I was meant for nothing. And I don't say that to suggest my life was meaningless or I did not do sometimes great or good or worthy things. Just that, like others before me, I was told I could be put to purpose. Which meant the living of every day without purpose was meaningless. Which meant I created meaning to be purposeful and created purpose to be valuable.

I don't deny the desire to be valuable or purposeful. But I won't lie and say these are finite or concrete things that are measurable or inherent. I don't see this as the power my consumer wanted.

When he saw me, he saw something out of a catalog. Mother of two loading groceries into a car. That is when I first felt someone watching, the hint of being seen in a way I'd never been seen before. And the two little ones are okay. I know this because after the initial stun and ache to my senses in the grocery store parking lot, I could hear him turn on the A/C in my van before closing them in. It was hot out, I believe. It's hard to remember now. Not the details, but what hot is. What it means or feels like. Everything feels hot and cold now just as you'd expect it to in space.

The news confirmed the children were safe and this meant a great working chain in me could stop its twisting and the slack made it easy to give up entirely. If I say I am nothing without my children, you will feel sad for me or think me powerless. I simply mean, we are all nothing without our imagined purposes. And my purpose in those moments was in the arms of their father who was backed by our crying, worried, lost friends and family. And we had money and were white and there were no illnesses to hold us back. It was sickening actually, all our capability housed in our bodies and skin and bank. I don't feel sorry for us, not really. Though I had a few things left on my to-do list that day and a hidden wish for something salty and fatty to snack on later. And those things still bite at me—those things (more than others) make me feel the way I was left undone.

When the man hid in a corner and wept, I knew it would take much longer than I had hoped. I wouldn't tell anyone this—that I just wanted it over with. But there he was, a child in a corner. And I was a thing on a table. And there was nothing in between us but the past. Which sounds like I could have made a future if I tried a little harder—talked him out of it, talked him tired until I could free myself or wait out my own rescue.

Instead I thought of this strange little clearing in our yard when I was a child. My parents had bought the house and property and the land was overgrown with cattails and cottonwood trees and something that made my eyes itch. Among it all was a little clearing I found by chasing a kitten. In my memory, it was far from the house and the road and the driveway and no one could see me, but perhaps it was clear to adults where I spent my time. Dragging buckets and branches and rocks, making seats and tables for my farworld guests. Feeding the cat imaginary food in a real bowl, much to its madness. I built a world in that clearing, and when I was pulled from it for dinner or baths or chores or church or shopping or all the worst things in the world such as making new friends on the block, I would lock a part of myself away. All taut. This place where I had a world—still dangerous, but all mine.

There might have been hours on the table and the first were the ones of nerves and excuses (*maybe he made a mistake and will let me go*), followed by hours of acceptance and wetting myself and finding the bindings tight. And then the hours of waiting and nothing. Of what one might call giving up or giving in. It was in those hours that I finally felt normal. Perhaps this is why he thought me strong and why he rose from that corner. When I said I was finally where I always knew I'd be. We are all of us tied to slabs as we imagine the choices we make leading us further in life instead of closer to death.

I wonder if he saw this in me at the grocery store.

If I smelled . . . not weak, not a victim or lost or too vulnerable to the world, but aware of this hunt. Of the world's hunt. Women and girls know early on we must remember to survive. But most imagine themselves smart, strong, different, chosen, lucky, fortunate, blessed, wise, exceptional enough to avoid the claw and jaws. Most imagine themselves not as creatures, but as whole selves, thinking and feeling and rationalizing their way through the world. They plow and mow down overgrown landscapes and think they have tamed the wild.

Which is not to say that I really knew my destiny or that I am beyond or better than any of them. Just that sometimes I felt more animal than person. More space and emptiness and imagined life rather than what I was told I should see and believe. Perhaps he saw this when I was looking at a small jar of sweet pickles. The way I chuckled thinking about all the ways we try to dress up a cucumber. And when my youngest made a little doo-doo sound because she was getting used to her own voice, and her brother kissed her head as if her personhood was coming along so well and he was so proud and wouldn't we all be happy in the evening with our pickles and dinner.

Bah, maybe he saw none of this, just an opportunity. My back turned, the lot empty, a quiet day, the right day, a Tuesday. Something telling him *now*.

It's probably delusion that gives me the small satisfaction that I saw it coming. What pride there is in foresight. What satisfaction. The world an equation and not a mess of mishaps. The gurgles and choking. The body a shudder. He almost called out for help. Then the silence. I've nothing to say to my consumer when he arrives. I hear something shuffling and as his body grows cold and I can only walk along it as if on the edge of a cliff, I imagine it is him. *Where are we*, he will ask. Or, *what are we?* As if I should know. It will be like that moment before the knife sliced in, before the pain and the confusion, when we saw one another as we are. He was scared and bound to this solution of his and sorry, so sorry in his face and the slump of his shoulders and the way he kept looking away. And he didn't muster the strength until he saw it in me—I was bound to this solution too. Building imaginary lives in a clearing. We are nothing but his need to consume and my acceptance of all the ways humans are consumable. *It was almost a sacrifice*, I say to comfort myself. Us. *Almost.*

HEAVYWEIGHT IN TRAINING

Marie says it's not that hard. The nine months—no, she said it's actually ten. And everyone is out there taking care of you—well, the adults are. And strangers even. And yeah, some are assholes and stare, like the kids in our school stare, but really, it's just a giant chunk of one small year. Then it's over. And you can go about forgetting it and drinking and fucking and it's like it never happened.

"It's just like having a tough job. Then you quit."

Marie's lips are bright as those terrible pink awareness ribbons everyone is always wearing when they come over to see my mom. Marie smooths the gloss over her lips: top, then bottom, then top again. Lots of smacking and sliding her lips back and forth. Like she's working out the kinks. Like she's buffing out the dings. Her hair just-so, her clothes now fitted and tight against her hips. The gold and red leather bracelets don't scuff and rub raw, the way they do when I wear such things. Like championship belts, but for each of her svelte wrists. They barely move, and I can't imagine what happens to them if they dare pinch her.

"Everyone will talk, but everyone talks anyway. Fuck them. This old lady, Estelle, who works around the newborns at the hospital, came to my room and told me that. She said, 'You'll be different, but they won't. Fuck 'em!' An old lady said that to me. You're fine."

Marie leaves the bathroom, and I'm left pretending to primp in front of the mirror while trying to avoid looking at the heavy and loose billowing of my sweatshirt in my reflection. Robbie's sweatshirt. I barely know him, and he I, but it was left at the party and I put it on and didn't take it off and the more I traded my regular jeans for the scrappy wide-leg ones of my sister's, the more people wondered about that damn sweatshirt. I try not to wear it every day, and I put on my carefully curated outfit and think, "This will do." But by the time I reach the front door, I'm already back in Robbie's sweatshirt with that beer-sweat and boy smell and my clothes perfectly preserved underneath. And the more I forget it's there, the more Robbie's girlfriend Britney seems to care and is held by her tight group of beautiful friends so they are this spinning mob of "It's okay, Britney" that I have to avoid in the halls.

And I could just take it off and everyone could see me in my regular, fitted shirts, and they'd shut the fuck up about me and Robbie and why I'm "hiding" in his smelly clothes. But then I wouldn't have people like Marie talking to me. I've been in so many of her classes, and I've known her since grade school. And this is the first time she said my name and more than nodded. And I was stuck in her orbit for those few minutes in the bathroom wondering what it would be like to be pregnant and everyone knowing it. And all the parents, at first gossiping and *tsking*, but later opening doors and buying meals for me and letting me sit anywhere I wanted. I'd have this large part of myself that was not all myself, but a safe place for something partially of myself to grow. Grow big and out and then into the hands of some parents that spent their last dollars and hours and lives on some new thing to come in and grow big with them.

And people still snicker at Marie, and the stories are always floating around again, and it seems like the whole school doesn't know how Marie's face looks or how she's crafted her eyebrows to look "Mysterious Natural" from that online eyebrow-shaping guide, but they only notice the flatness of her stomach—because all they do is wait for it to bulge again. Even through all of that, there are still adults who don't know their words carry through the halls when talking about how brave she is and was.

She, a lone sibling now, when once there were years and years of her never alone. Then, BAM! She's it. She's the household. Everything runs around her schedule and needs and memories. Oh, her parents still doing whatever it is they do—or just her dad, I guess. Maybe she had a mom for a while. I don't really know the whole story. But her father no longer plans his time between her brother and her. "Sibb" means kinship, relationship, love, friendship, peace, happiness and now she, without it. Except when she finds it in someone else warming her and I can't imagine when she is kissed that her oh-so-pink lip color is in danger of smudging or rubbing off. Maybe it is, like when I walked in on Ruby and Matt making out at that party and his mouth was like a bruise from her dark red-black lipsticked lips. Marie, a brave girl. A strong girl. Who fell into the arms of someone to comfort her after the loss of her kinship-relationship-love-friendship-peace-n-happiness being. And me, with just a search history of entomology websites and horror stories.

They say the cancer cells divide and grow exponentially. They are uncontrollable. Everything else is just a barrier or net or take-a-deep-breath-and-see process. Old English says "cancer" is a spreading sore, and underneath it or around it or holding it or being swallowed by it is my mom. The stacks of things are piling up around her. All the flowers and gifts and the neighbors calling and dropping things off for her and for us. And my mom is too nice to say "Fuck them," so instead someone like Maudell can just walk into our house and filch her gifts. Even our little poodle Max is afraid of Maudell, and Max is the warmest, cuddliest friend I have along with this god-awful sweatshirt that Marie would never be caught dead in, even when she was pregnant and bulging.

I remember Robbie setting the beer-wet sweatshirt down on the edge of the couch. His hair was rustled and his eyelids were heavy and any minute they would have slammed shut. He was holding his car keys and some other jock assholes were telling him not to drive. And he was telling them to "cool it, just cool it" and readying his legs so he could just stand there like he does on the field: a wall. And those boys were smelling of defeat because all the other girls besides me had found a guy or girl to pull into a dark corner or empty room already. I remember thinking this is the scenario that everyone says to avoid: being the only girl at a party with big asshole drunk dudes. But they barely saw me there and I'm sure they wouldn't have seen me even if I was making my lips sparkly pink or thrusting my hip out as I teased one of them about . . . whatever it is they want to be teased about. How stupid Joe Bendel is because he can't get that DNA has only four chemical bases? Is that what he wants to be teased about?

Anyway, there they were: Robbie, Joe Bendel, and two other guys and they looked like they were just playing and roughhousing, but it seemed like it went a couple seconds too long, a couple pounds too much. I remember thinking it's not just me and the beer and the weed, but that something in the air had changed and these guys were no longer numbers on the football team or people with lockers full of half-assed assignments and books never opened at school and nothing to say in class. They were a tangle of muscles, grunts, and determination. The end table and items on the fireplace mantle near them were in danger of dropping to the ground and not cracking or shattering, but bumping about and showing their own weight as they rocked back and forth. I couldn't tell which of the other boys were which, but I could see Robbie and how quickly he would scramble when one got what seemed like a solid hold on him. His bulk never betrayed him the way I expected it to. The way my dad always watched the heavy-weights instead of the welterweights because he said the bigger guys were strong, but had to know how to keep themselves in check unless their weight betrays them. When one guy would go for the hips and another for the shoulders, I thought he was done. I thought Robbie would be on the floor and those keys taken from his hands, and he'd say "I give" or just angry-laugh or get mad and storm off into the kitchen and shotgun another beer. I thought I'd see that. I thought I'd see someone lose, someone say "Enough," and someone just stop trying finally. Stop trying to get out and away and who the fuck cares if he shouldn't be driving, he'd do so, and he would be fine the way everyone at my school is always buzzed and driving and fine. And maybe if he wasn't, he'd hit a tree and splat and the only people to give a fuck would be the ones wishing they could change things that they could never change in the first place because the joke is always on them to think they could control all the spreading of sores and raiding cells in a body or in a high school or in all the ways everyone had something or other to say about Marie, the "slut-bag."

But he didn't stop and he wouldn't, and soon enough one of the boys went tumbling back towards the fireplace, and the sound of his head hitting the mantle was louder than the grunting and heavy breathing. Of course, I was the only one that wasn't frozen on the spot and the one that inspected that silly knock to his head and made the call that we just needed some ice and something to wipe up the blood and someone to stay up with him until he could go home safely. And Robbie slumped down on the couch, not done and not yet defeated, but tired still. And he threw the sweatshirt out of his way and next to me and he said he would keep me and the other guy company. "You're Julie—Juliette, right?" he said, but then he drifted off to sleep and continued to twitch and readjust his shoulders for the next three or so hours until the injured kid felt well enough to call his mom to come pick him up, hoping he wouldn't get yelled at too badly and promising that none of us would get in trouble.

When Ruby showed back up at her own party from the mouthy jumble and pawing hands-under-the-clothes session with Matt, she saw the mess in the living room and the sopping towel from the melted ice, pink with blood run thin, and she freaked as one would expect. Instead of hopping up to calm her down and talk her through how not-bad it all really was and why her life was a mess, I just pretended I had maybe dozed off, and I pulled Robbie's sweatshirt around me. And he didn't ask for it back. Not then, not now.

And if people want to talk about how my mom's dying slowly as if we are perpetually in a hospital room with my mom hooked up to some machine beeping and my eyes not puffy but with long strands of tears down my cheeks, as if we were not actually just . . . living with this, they'll do it anyway. And if they say these big baggy clothes of mine are indicators that I've followed in Marie's slut-bag's footsteps and that I'm either going to be a saint for bringing a baby to the world for some sad-ass couple or that I'm a fuck-up and acting out from the danger of losing my mom, then whatever. Whatever.

The truth is I'm still a virgin, watching boring movies about kids preparing to give it away at proms and on special love-tight moments and with their super-hot, supernatural boyfriends. And the pile of my biology project sits at home at the end of my desk as untouched as I am, and I have to decide if I'm going to go to class anyway and pretend my project is well on its way for tomorrow's due date or if I'll really just calm the fuck down and focus and finish it probably by 4 a.m. tonight. Or if (and more likely) I'll shuffle up to Mr. Gershwin and allow him to look me up and down and make internal notes about my ratty clothes and possibly bulging belly, and he'll think of some Hollywood version of my sick mother and nod "yes" before I even finish asking for an extension.

THE KILLERS OF RABBITS AND BROTHERS

L innea's rabbit is dead.

Not the dead of her grandmother that meant she had become invisible. Not the dead of her brother that kept her mother too exhausted to continue weeping. It was the dead of things stiff and blood-streaked and plain as day. She pokes at Bunny several more times with the stick and only manages to bother the surrounding flies for a second or two before they land and lift off the mangled flesh busy and pleased.

Linnea knows what it is like for her family to get bad news. She knows they will fall into their seats and beds and when they move it is only to shift the objects around them from one place to another. To hand off the daily makings of a life. Her family talks in words that no longer hold anything but thuds and whimpers. To receive bad news, to know of the dead, means to live under an awfulness. And seven-year-old Linnea would not be a harbinger of awfulness today. At least, not to her dear mom and dad.

The truth is Bunny had also seemed to be in what was called "mourning" around the house. Brad, who was a sometimes loud and rowdy older brother, and a little cruel with Linnea's other possessions, was always gentle with Bunny. Even talked to her a bit with a softness Linnea rarely heard. Until, of course, the group of boys showed up and taunted him out of her world and into another one of consuming all the contents of the fridge, smelling of bodies and stuffed heat, and the pushing, shoving of one another out the door. They could never just walk along together, but created a sequence of action and reaction. And loudness. The silence that followed them was a welcome emptying of time and space.

Linnea leans closer to Bunny to inspect its one open eye. The wide darkness it once held seems as dull as its fur. Not matted and bloody, but as if a great smudge was left inside it. Bunny wouldn't mind Linnea's careful inspection of her body. Many afternoons were spent with Bunny as patient, as baby, as detective companion. Linnea knows the weight and dimensions of her rabbit. She knows the bumps and plump bits. And Linnea detected a crushing of sorts had happened. As she moves the fur around with small sticks and even a flat rock, she can see most of Bunny is still there. Not eaten. No puncture marks. Instead, where a roundness in Bunny should be, there is just a sunkenness and the blood from some sort of blunt pounding. And bubbles around the mouth. It isn't unlike Linnea to notice such things, having lived on a ranch and never being shooed away from all acts of nature and man. And rowdy boys.

One might say after having buried the body of Bunny, Linnea sits quietly against a great cottonwood tree thinking of her friend as if waiting for someone. One might want to say Linnea is put in the path of another certain jackrabbit perhaps by the hand of God or angels. Perhaps there is a grand system of the cosmos that often puts the heartbroken within touch of a listening ear—any listening ear. But saying so would mean we'd have to ignore the careful path this rabbit took in following the girl from Bunny's crime scene to her burial. One would need to ignore the rabbit's keen sense of things broken and unkind. And more importantly, we'd have to believe rabbits aren't astute creatures of justice and harbingers of vengeance.

The truth is jackrabbits believe in a graceful balance of good and evil. When they look to be things of fluff and sweetness, they are actually fast and shrewd. The trembling and twitching that is mistaken for fear is only a ruse, for when they fight, they do so on their hind legs with quick jabs and the mobility of a featherweight. Rarely do they need to exhibit this prowess because they will be mistaken for weak things, and this gets them very far in life. It even keeps a young girl from startling or screaming when a rabbit with horned growths upon its head approaches.

Linnea's brother and his rowdy friends had once told her stories of jackalopes and the games they play. But Linnea is never one to be teased or duped and as the town vet had once cleaned Bunny's ears and checked her nose, he answered her question and explained cottontail rabbits are susceptible to a certain virus that results in growths of keratin, the same things her hair and nails were made of, on their "little bunny heads" (which were his words, not hers). The vet may have told her to keep clear of such animals as they are infected with Shope papilloma, at which point Linnea reasoned she wouldn't need to bother because a wild rabbit would never let her get that close to it unless it had its own motivations. And in this case, it did.

Linnea doesn't even need to bother hearing the rabbit's version of what happened to Bunny. Its two twitches of the nose are a signal to Linnea. As she begins describing the rowdy brothers—the very ones that taunted her brother to swim far too long a distance across far too fast of a river—she can simply tell the rabbit knows the very ones. The ones with homemade slingshots who set empty cans along a busted fence for target practice. They'd bustle through the meadow thinking no one can hear the howls and laughter. They'd talk of girls as bitches and when one would show a thinner skin, he'd immediately be pounced upon into a dog pile of insults and wrestling. These boys were now quick to apologize and look away when they neared her screaming drunk father in town. Always ducking into some fake busy life when they saw her. Look at the phone. Look at this interesting piece of nothing on the sidewalk. Look at this thing on my hand, my skin because maybe in the lower layers of dermis there is an answer for the guilty. The rowdy boys: Brody, James, Jonas, and Christian. Killers of rabbits and brothers.

The camping trip was Brody's idea, and while everyone knew they weren't going to where they were before, when they lost their pack member Brad, they all agreed on a place close enough. Close enough to not pretend it didn't happen, but not right there. Never right there. It is strange how none of them can last more than twenty minutes apart. When the body didn't resurface and there was nothing but the rush of water and the birds fussing over a new scent in the air, they had looked upon one another as strangers. No recognition of who they once were as if they'd been transported into a realm where iffy possibilities increased into *probably*s and *certainly*s and, finally, *always*. Always, Brad didn't resurface on his own. Always, the water rushed on. Always, they were goaders of catastrophe. When each found himself alone, there was something in the body that revolted. An electric surge that came in jolts and pulses to the blood. Get out. Move. The cells screamed and refused to downshift. There was no settling anymore.

They hate one another and need to see each other regularly in order to keep that hate alive. It is easier knowing one can hate himself as long as he is hated back. They shove the camping supplies around with a little more force than usual. They dump things on the ground with an added impact of frustration. They snap and bicker and as long as each of them feel the whip of another, they can continue putting up their campground, building a fire, and opening warm stolen beers. They talk, but no one says much. James is the first to think of mentioning Brad. Something funny he had said once. What was it? Another would have remembered the whole line. Someone else the context. But James and the others keep Brad stories and remember whens far from reach.

"I hate camping," James says, which isn't true but seems like the thing to say. The boys nod. The fire begins to smolder and the dozing off here and there turns into hefty snores. No one bothers to move into the tent, but instead they sleep on a hard ground that sucks up their heat.

James hears it first. Like a clearing of a throat or a muffled cough. It can't be Brad's because Brad is dead but it seems just like the often-annoying tic he had right before suggesting something stupid or awful or too generous for a boy of fifteen. James pulls the sleeping bag over his head until he hears it again.

"Hey," Brody says almost to himself. Then again to the sleeping forms around him.

"Yeah. I heard it," James says.

Christian sits up abruptly when the noise gets louder. Jonas, as always, follows. It is more than a clearing of a throat now. There is a word or two in there. Too jumbled to hear, but so close. Close enough.

"Who's there?"

"Brody, shh!" James says. The voice seems to be coming from different places around them. It beckons. "Come here" or "Come" or "One." The others still can't make out the words, but know they won't be staying in their sleeping bags for long.

"Somebody fucking with us?" Jonas whispers.

"Get bent!" Brody yells. His voice falters at the end, having tried on a voice he never had before.

"Bent?" James mouths. Brody's shrug is one of vultures, head jutted, shoulders raised, eyes hard and animal.

A stirring, almost a footstep. Almost a repositioning or even a movement towards them.

"Get help," the voice says, which is enough for Jonas and Christian to forget about tying up their laces.

"I'm going to find out what the fuck is going on," Christian says. He smacks his flashlight twice against his palm and watches the beam slice through the air.

"Get that out of my face," James says, half-pretending to get outside of his sleeping bag. Brody has already begun working the bag down his legs, his feet finally shoving the thing in a clump nearer to the smoking logs of the fire.

"Help," the voice says.

Both Jonas and Christian take off. Quick at first to the edge of the camping area, but then slowly edging through the brush. James hears them for what seems like a few minutes before the shuffle of Brody getting his shoes on drowns out the area.

"I'm getting out of here."

"Don't leave us."

"Then hurry up. It's probably nothing anyway."

But James can't get himself up and to the truck. He can't imagine the drive along the dirt road without nightmaring something jumping out in front of them. He doesn't want to think of Jonas and Christian's parents' faces. That arrested look. Disbelief. While Brody often thought of the way Brad's mother's face frowned—the whole face, like a worming pumpkin—James only remembers the unbelieving faces. *Surely this is a mistake. I'll call him myself.* Brad never answering.

As Brody's truck stalls twice on its way out of the campground, James finally stands up and starts towards the edge of the clearing.

The jackalopes' horns are not unreal. In fact, the very scleroprotein that makes up those growths means "horn-like" in Greek. Keratin. We are not to forget the firm chain-like grip those long scleroprotein filaments make when they reach across things soluble and active. They bond. A careful double coiling of rods locked together makes human hair and nails as well as parts of our own skin. In reptiles, birds, and amphibians, keratin bundles make a tougher unmineralized tissue: the shell, scales, feathers, and beaks.

The horn-like growths on the rabbit are not easy or graceful in their development. It is of the same genetic make-up that offers our skin as protection, which allows us to feel sensations and to regulate our own temperature. We live because of our skin organ and our skin exists because of keratin. But the reckless growth of hardened keratin tumors can take over the entire face of the rabbit infected with the Shope papilloma virus. Perhaps along the mouth, cheeks, and even the soft roll of dewlap.

Keratin doubles in length and strength each week. In that amount of time, human nails grow from 0.5 millimeters to 1.2 millimeters. The longest nails of a male recorded at 32 feet, 3.8 inches long. They more than coiled and twisted around themselves, they weighed down the fingers and hands of the owner, causing chronic cramping and eventual disfigurement. A single strand of hair can potentially hold up to 100 grams. In theory, a whole head of hair could endure between 12,345–18,518 pounds. The acrobatic hair hangers are just a hint to this possibility. Keratin makes this so.

The protein is relentless and to James, it is deadly. When he first sees the jackalope, he imagines his face must look like that of Brad's father that day: shocked still. Carved into a moment of time forever. This small furry thing before him is the size and shape of the rabbit they had killed just yesterday. They pelted rocks at it with their newest slingshot and when they assumed it was dead, they rushed to its side. But it was still breathing, barely and in hard-earned huffs. Brody had been the one to put a larger rock to it. "Out of its misery," he had breathed. The boys felt relieved.

But the familiarity ends at the size and shape. The horns on the rabbit are uneven and crude. Not the elegant slope of an elk or pronghorn nor even the tidy, but impressive horns on the stuffed jackalopes in town. The rabbit boasts a tangle of hardened black prongs, at times looking more like mangled branches of a tree than antler. They gather along the top of the rabbit's head, with some near the mouth like tusks.

At first, James assumes the prickle under his skin is from nerve confusion, having learned he isn't in fact facing anything from a bobcat to a serial killer or even Brad's drunk and angry father in the woods taunting the boys to their death. Instead, it is an antlered-rabbit, once mythic or supernatural, but now just vulgar and diseased.

And determined.

Soon the prickle builds into a buzz of cellular activity. As the rabbit keeps its ground, its nose still the cute twitching thing of every childhood story, the keratin James' body houses extends its once sensible reach from one monomer to many. James trembles and begins to scratch at himself. The keratin doubling and tripling the filaments, filling itself up and pushing out the cellular filling and buffers into a cellular compost of types. He can feel it first in his nails. The growth of the nail so quick that the nailbed has no time to detach itself from the deadening nail. His skin raw and bleeding in pinpricks until the space of the nailbed is just too small and like a hangnail, it begins slicing its way into the sides of the fingers and then down each phalange. The nail extends almost inches now, almost half a foot, leaving a pulp of flesh and blood and dead cells where his hand used to be.

Where the skin doesn't tear as his fingernails and now toenails had, the water and fluids of his epidermis begin to flee their settled places. A slickness covers most of his arms and legs, chest, neck and face, and soon the softer parts of his body: the belly, under his arms and the insides of his thighs, to his groin and rectum. Slick like a thin pus, almost just a warmth rather than fluid. The water is pushed out by the work of keratin in his stratum spinosum. Filament by filament it fills this lofty layer of his epidermis so there is no room but atop and below it. The hardening of the skin works both ways: a type of shell or scales building up and out of the skin as well as cutting down below into the subcutaneous level—snapping nerve receptors and glands along the way. Had he fingers left, he'd instinctively reach for his forearm hoping to both hold his keratin in and keep it from its new jagged reach to his bone.

Finally, it isn't the hair on top of his head that does him in. While the rest of the body spasms, dissected by its own protein spilling forth and in, the hair on his head grows as much as expected. Forcing its way through his scalp. The splotches of facial hair work into a new toughness and wind its way through its own forest of spiked tumors. While his entire body feels only of things gone rigid, like caked mud drying but from the inside out, it is the skin inside his nose that his body's shock will not ignore. The small hair follicles along the lateral nasal wall don't explode with the protective protein as the others have. Instead it is like an unending flooding of keratin, a suffocation of the secretory cavity. Like the first quick seconds when Brad felt the water plow through his nose and throat. Like the first quick seconds Bunny scrounged around her lungs for air only to find an ooze escaping her. The follicles vibrate and twist around to hold in the keratin protein as it builds and builds. No bit of nature or man would force itself into

James the same way Bunny and Brad had died, but instead it would plunge its way out of his skin. The jagged, robust horn-like tumors burst through his septum and skull, a tangle of strong-willed cells to destroy what weak a thing James turned out to be and—to rabbit and Linnea's great pleasure—to defend the kinder things of this world.

INTO A BETTER-THAN-NOTHING

Penny Davis imagined wire holding her smile in place. Space wire. Titanium folded over itself one hundred times, but small as a wisp of hair, sewn through the corners of her mouth up into the inside of her own cheeks. Her teeth, a dock of some kind for the pile of lip stocked there. Too bright, too white teeth. Too big of a smile. Her eyes, giant and the blue-grey color of molding fruit, or the grey-blue of a blue heron when Penny was in the right light and wearing a complementary scarf or headband.

In the white heat of the filming lamps with her too big smile stuck to her face, Penny couldn't imagine if her eyes were blue-grey or grey-blue and somehow this detail felt massive and her arms continued to shake in an effort to fall down to her sides from the disciplined pose she had locked them into. She didn't dare unlock. The bodies around her, the arms above them, the fingers aligned and palms slightly cupped. The sky more than a sky but a thick black matte paper that she had expected would shrivel or disintegrate in order to reveal His light behind it. She had expected the stars to turn in on themselves or burst like fireworks as the day shone brighter than the cold, immense night. The remaining Cult of Tomorrow's Tomorrow swarmed in the hillside. The cameras followed them as they spun slowly imagining their robes turned from the itchy cotton blend they were into a heat—into a light or into a better-than-nothing. They imagined bodies warming in the coldest places and the ache of bare heels gaining a sense of water. As if floating. As if the body was always made of the water of His love.

Penny Davis continued to smile. Continued to spin. Continued, with her arms quivering above her head. Not looking around. Not flinching when one of the cameramen mouthed "12:31."

Penny moved closer to Louisa Goodly. Louisa's arms appeared not to tremble. Her smile, natural and relaxed. Louisa shook her head and bent her arms, head, and upper torso toward Penny Davis.

"It's happening!" Louisa said. Her body swayed back to place as if it had been only a wind that had wished her to speak to Penny.

"It's happening!" Louisa Goodly sung.

"It's happening!" Charma Able repeated.

Penny didn't dare move her face toward the ladies but pulled the wires within her smile tighter. Goodly. Able. The others: Judy Goodman. Talia Light. Patty Fuller. Marsha Love. Wendy White. She was just Penny Davis. Just a Davis. Goodman, Love, and White swam toward one another, never making eye contact. Their hips guiding them. The head as if an afterthought moving with the current. Only Light and Fuller stayed near Brady. His body, a titan planet. They rotated around him, careful not to ambush one another's revolution.

A camera moved closer to Penny. "12:42," someone said, and as the women chanted "It's happening! It's happening!" Brady M. Hagar began murmuring. He closed his eyes and pulled his elbows closer to his body. His forearms to his fingertips, a fountain. He motioned for all to come closer to him and the soft whisper of words began to pick up.

"We've been blessed, my children!" He said.

The cameras closed in on him and the increasingly tight radius of the group. With only a second of time to look away from the heavens and towards Brady, Penny Davis saw the bodies and partially obscured faces of the cameramen. For each man, one eye was closed and the other always lost to the machine that jutted in front of it and settled on the shoulder. Both hands were used to steady the camera and only the stance of each and the shape of the mouth and chin was available for Penny to see. They stood solid. Both feet flat. No swaying of hips or torso. They looked as secure in standing as they might be if they suddenly leapt forward or away. Or up. The mouth of each was caught in a twist. One man's bottom lip looked swallowed by his mouth. The top teeth guarding any entry or escape. Another's cheeks were sagged, so low the jaw fell with it. The lips remained touching, hiding as best it could this lull of skeletal structure. Penny Davis thought to look for the director, the bulk of man who bustled his crew around the farm and schoolhouse. The one that had said nothing yesterday as a string of bodies, small and tall, old and young, slouched and walked towards the front gate of the farm.

Brady had waved the marching group on and blessed them in front of the cameras, but they only marched faster, a sloppy troop avoiding eye contact.

"We will not see you in heaven, my brother and sisters. But the Lord's love will reach you as best it can! Look for breaks in the darkness like you would a falling star and know that the disciples of Tomorrow's Tomorrow will be thinking of you as we are raised closer to our Lord and away from the sins and inequities of this terrestrial plane!"

Brady moved among the remaining eight women in Tomorrow's Tomorrow, his murmur sped and increased in volume as they neared him. Penny tried to smell him, the him underneath the hay and sweat that wafted from his body. She tried to detect the wooded smell of him. The one she encountered on her nights as his Today Wife. Like the smell of her family home when her father had still lived there. She tried to lean in closer to him, but the floating ease of Louisa Goodly moved between them.

"I can feel it!" Louisa sang.

"I can feel it!" the other women joined in.

Penny tried mouthing the words, but only too late as a camera lens moved toward her face. She dared not look into it. Dared not let loose the wires, dare not relax her smile.

Brady's eyes remained shut, but Penny knew he felt the distance of each woman and each camera from him. The same way he knew the men of Tomorrow's Tomorrow were within days of removing him. He saw them the same way He saw everything, he said. His sight is not the sight of eyes, but of the heart.

"My sight is not the sight of eyes, but of the heart, Penny," He had said when she arrived at the ranch. "The sight of the soul. And the soul does not live in any one time. The soul lives all at once and forever. It can't understand a past or a tomorrow. But only the tomorrow of tomorrow, Penny. Your past means only your path to your new home—to me."

As the small group continued to swoon closer together, Penny thought of her family and her childhood home for the first time in many months. She remembered the smell of burnt butter as her mom forgot the heated saucepan on the stove. She remembered the 3-1-1-2 rhythm of descending the large staircase; she liked to start it fast and slow the jumps down as she tapped twice the portrait of her Grandma and Grandpa Davis that hung on the wall to her left. The final two quick jumps ended in a stomp at the bottom of the stairs, her mom howling from the pantry for her to knock it off. Penny Davis remembered her friends, Johnny and Angie Bell. The sprints to the gate before the school bus arrived. The afternoon light on her schoolbooks when she napped on the porch. The deep smack of her mama's paddle and the wet eyes of Johnny when his family sent him away from her and her growing belly. Penny wondered where her daughter was. Her last memory was of the child marching in that line with her Yesterday

Husband. The no looking back and her three-year-old's misplaced step that didn't end with little Molly falling up into the steps of the bus. Her stepfather had scooped her up at the last minute. No tears. No thoughts of would-be scraped knees or broken lips. Just away.

Brady was then upon her, His breath along her neck and the back of her ears, the heat of his chest near her shoulders. "We've been saved," he said to only her. Penny Davis could feel the weight of him on her again. Her first night as his Today Wife, she'd been afraid He'd feel the wornness of her—"It's like fucking an old dishrag!" her father had once yelled to her mother. Penny had turned over, pulled her arms closer to her chest, lifted her hips and thighs closer to him and pushed her face into the soft threadbare pillow on the bed. "You'll be saved," He had said that night. The force of him driving the memory of her father, the 3-1-1-2 staircase, and her mother's laughter out of her head.

"Saved!" Penny sang.

"Saved!" the women repeated.

Brady murmured and hallallujah'd to the sky. The titanium space wire of Penny's smile snapped back into place. Her eyes the blue-grey color of a blue heron and wet with a slickness and relief. She swayed to the sound of the bodies around her. She dodged the clever Louisa Goodly's step in front of the camera and Penny Davis dropped her shoulders and head coyly to the right. She stared straight into the lens of the camera. Still young and dewy, the first raindrop full and wet on a spider's web.

"Saved," she mouthed and winked at the grimacing face behind the lens.

DID YOU FIND YOUR KILLER YET?

When DeDeAnne's body was found, the town became nothing but a wail. It began in the family dining room, where all the piles of *Lost Child* flyers took residence on the scratched pine table. The neighbor women and family friends and one half-sister of De-DeAnne's mom began to wail as well—some inside the mouth, under the tongue, some aloud in words like "There, there," and "Someone should really . . ." The wail grew to the rest of the family, the rest of the street, and down through the soil so that once anyone reached the small town, they too became part of it.

When DeDeAnne's body was found, the town was a wail except for in one solitary person. She was indeed the last to know of the incident. For when DeDeAnne died, no one remembered to tell her. She wasn't a ghost. She wasn't a memory birthed back into life. She was flesh and bone and all the things a living young girl should be.

At first, DeDeAnne thought it might be a game.

"Not now, DeDe," they said to her when she tugged at arms and declared herself. "Not now," they said again, a little meat in the voice, a little gruff, a little substantive. When the detective faced her parents and held his hands in front of him, then behind his back, and then at his sides screaming for them to stay still, DeDe hopped and ran in circles in front of him. Nothing. Her parents had become strange anchors on the couch. As if the world was a sea. As if the water had filled their lungs and only songs of seaweed and crustaceans bubbled in their brains. The detective stood, her parents stayed on the couch, and a family therapist leaned into the scene from a puffy, floral-patterned chair. The family cat stretched, claws nearly stuck in the couch leg, only to pull the claws loose and close again, up and under its body, lost to the fluff and black-gray swirl of itself.

DeDeAnne insisted she was not dead. And each in turn said "Not now."

Once the detective retreated, the therapist went to the kitchen to make tea, lean against the counter, rub her stubby fingers into her eye, and push away her desire to text her not-yet-boyfriend with something about this tragedy—a partial invitation so he could say something meaningful, heartfelt, soulmate-like to her, or so she could pretend it was never an invitation to begin with in case he didn't. "Not now," she said to DeDe. She hit send and waited for her phone's screen to go black.

"If not now, then when?" DeDe said in her best almost-mature voice, the one she picked up from a girl two years older down the street. *If not now, when?* She practiced the words a few more times. They were good ones, the kind that unlock something in adults, like great vault doors giving way to a future made present.

"Fine," said the therapist, "but we've only to talk about this once. We can't be wasting time, when there's so much more to do like address the anger and the bargaining and the floral arrangements.

"Tulips," the therapist mouthed and turned her head to the not-now girl.

"Well, I'm not dead," DeDeAnne said. She put her hands on her hips. She put her chin at a tilt to the right. And she refused to lose any eye contact with the therapist.

"Have you heard of denial?" the therapist asked.

"I'm here and you can touch me and this is flesh and blood and the words are coming out of my mouth and you can hear them and I can feel myself growing. I can feel my cells holding a secret of tomorrow and the tomorrow after that."

"Sure, but what of it, when you were so young—too young," said the therapist. She looked at her phone. "You never even got to kiss someone. Oh—but what that man probably did . . ."

The therapist's shoulders and chest made several shudders and she blinked a thousand times and her thoughts were bulldozed back into a landfill.

"I'm not dead and nothing bad happened to me."

"Such a brave girl," the therapist said and finally let go of the counter and quarter-turned to lean down to DeDe. "We have to accept many things in this world, brave girls or not. I'm accepting things right now. I've no texts from my maybe-boyfriend, no new shoes for the funeral service, no desire to talk to a stupid little dead thing that can't be bothered to see how it is and lie still—so—even if it is true that you'll continue to grow, you'll have to accept this very hard thing too. Brave and smart and idiotic and trusting and head-of-fluff girls die. All the time. In horrible ways. The world is cruel.

"Acceptance," the therapist whispered and turned to finish making all the tea, check her phone, count the amount of tea bags left in the cupboard, check her phone, tidy her mess, and push herself back into the front room and back to the wail.

DeDeAnne couldn't imagine following her and entering that space yet again, hearing that wail from her mother's hip. It was the only part of her mother that had not developed a hint of sound before. It was a quiet place, her mother's hip, where she balanced DeDeAnne as a baby, as a toddler, and once as a kid who clung to her when she burned her finger. The mother's hip remembered the weight of the child, remembered the slight thrust it needed to balance the child while her other arm was free to fight the world from her.

The doctor's office was the smell of staleness and sweat and tired on top of the smell of things sterile and Clorox and anti-everything, all of which was coated in the smell of choked flowers from a spray can. The doctor typed notes into the computer from a yellow notepad and each hit of the space bar was deliberate and produced a clack that filled the room. DeDe tried her best not to interrupt too loudly as Dr. Jens had always been a warm and solid entity within DeDe's life, despite what others continued to say.

"Not now," the doctor said and brushed at a small tear developing in the eye. "Your body was so cold. Just so cold. Even under that sheet. And not the TV blue of corpses I had readied myself for. It was a loss of blue and a loss of color all together even in that once-dark skin of yours."

"Well, you can touch my arm now, if you'd like."

"It wouldn't help. The blood moving through you, the flesh that is storing its secrets, and the bone that continues spewing out its coding matters very little right now. You are gone to us, DeDeAnne. Gone gone gone. The way of things tossed away."

"I don't feel tossed away. I don't feel gone, Doctor."

"It matters little. When they found your body it was all the stuff of nightmares, you know. What with the song atmospheric and sobering in the background while the sun went down and the volunteers flushed themselves throughout the forest. The soft glow of flashlights bopping about. And then the shouts were heard and the detective, looking ragged-angry, still sure-footed his way over. It was all very dramatic. By the time I got there, the sun was back up and though I shouldn't have, I just kept saying 'Who would do this? Who could do such a thing?' Of course, the autopsy would prove it, you know. Blunt force and whatnot. Ligature marks and whatnot. Here, I wrote it on this paper."

DeDe grabbed the doctor's yellow pad to see 'Blunt force and whatnot. Ligature marks and whatnot. Time of death TBA,' scrawled in green pen.

"The detective will say it was pre-meditated, of course. When you were just sleeping or at school or looking at cans of SpaghettiOs at the grocery story, this future was unspooling out in front of you. People have died here, of course. But you, so young. Who could do such a thing? The stuff of nightmares."

DeDe shook her head. She felt deep inside herself, tried to meditate on her liver and spine. She tried to listen to her veins and nothing in her felt dead at all. Nothing felt silent. She was thrumming and awake.

As she rode her bike to the police station, her legs and heart were pumping a certainty through her. Her blood was hers. Her air was hers. There was nothing between the world and her, until she saw the first townsperson, and then another, and another. She braced herself. *See me. See me breathing.* She waved, but a chorus of *Not now* followed her. The townsfolk *tsked* and shook at her, exhausted from oh-so-much-death-in-the-world.

Her own friends rolled towards her from the playground field to the street, like so many wayward playground rubber balls of the past. "Point him out!" they chanted at her. "Point him out!" Even Charlie motioned for her to stop, and when she did, he kept his hand on her hand. "You could just point out your killer, DeDe. And then we could tell someone for you. We couldn't keep this secret. We wouldn't be afraid. We'd tell our parents—unless it's our parents. Is it our parents, DeDe? Did our parents kill you?" he cried.

DeDe brushed his hand off hers and continued down the street. "Not yet," she began to scream. "I'm not dead yet," she yelled, hoping to shut down that terrible wail in the town.

"Of course you are," said the detective. He was sitting on a bench near the police station eating a salad from a paper bag. "I know. I should be eating a hot dog or burger or a sub," he said to her, "but this case has me not sleeping, not feeling well. Not shitting either." He fluffed the lettuce about. "Roughage," he whispered.

DeDe left her bike splayed out in the sidewalk as she half-nodded.

"Aren't you too busy to talk to me?" she asked in a voice that was not even like her own. A tiny one.

"It's fine. All I do is talk to the dead and the missing and the things gone." The detective spit out a still-yellow cherry tomato. "God, that sounds more interesting than it is."

"Well, I'm not dead."

"Well, we found your body."

"My body is right here." She put an arm out, which he reached for reluctantly, sadly, and with the "mmhhm" of one resigned to his job.

"Fair enough," he said. He let go of her wrist, and for a second wished he could keep that warm of her on his fingertips. Grab her up and place her in custody. He got this way with all the children in the town when he thought of all the awful in the world. Put them under surveillance. And lock. And key.

"The kid cases are always the hardest," he said. Then he pulled out his small notepad and read the words. "Yeah, that's right. 'The kid cases are always the hardest.'"

"The therapist said I could still grow and the doctor didn't say I was a ghost or memory either. I think I'm alive, detective. I think I'm still here. I know I am. Could a dead person do this?" She kicked the detective in the shin, once softly and once more thinking of soccer balls, and misplaced rocks on otherwise clear paths, and the way the one neighbor kid had kicked that wishful dog.

"Ouch. Well, I normally wouldn't think a dead person could kick me. I really wouldn't. And if you were a ghost, you could probably help save this case. And if you were a memory, I think I wouldn't care so much about this half-eaten salad.

"Bad tomatoes," he mouthed before continuing. "But, let's say you are alive, what is there even to do?"

"You could tell my parents. And everyone."

"Hmm, I don't know. We've just been through so much already. Finding your body like that. The stuff of nightmares.

"Did I get that right?" he asked and pulled the notepad out of his pocket again. "Here it is, yep yep. 'The stuff of nightmares.'"

"Maybe you should take me there, then. To where you found me."

"Oh, it matters little. It's a field, of course. A field and there's some woods nearby. And it was at the end of everything. And we looked for footprints and tire tracks. And we talked about access roads. And the town therapist isn't very good at profiling, but one of the volunteers offered up some thoughts on the dump site." He caught himself still talking to someone. "Oh, I'm sorry. That's what it was, you were dumped there. As you know."

"I really don't."

"Well, there didn't seem to be any struggle or anything in the area to suggest the deed was done there. Nope, you were snatched or invited somewhere else and then—then all the things of our nightmares playing out—and then your body there in the field where we found you. It happens like that, you know. Well, that's what I hear. Hold on—yep, here. I wrote it down. 'Find in a field. Call it a dump site.' I'm on the mark today."

"Does it say anything else? About catching the guy? Or about what becomes of my life?"

"Oh, well, the wail will quiet down eventually, I think. Though there will be moments when people remember you. Your parents must sit themselves still sometimes. And sometimes even acquaintances will suddenly think of you. They'll be sad and think about how it could have happened to their own. Oh, and my investigation will lead me to a family member, a weirdo in the town, then the last person we ever thought of, then to myself, and then to the woods where there will be a story about what lies buried in there. And then possibly to your doctor who will, of course, suffer at the hands of someone seeking justice, only to find it was not the doctor. And then I think back around to that neighbor kid who kicked the dog. Sometimes I might think it is a stranger, an outsider. Wouldn't that be something? Out of nowhere, right? Catching a serial killer," he said and dreamed the dream of putting a small town and its small-town cop on the map. "Gah, it matters little anyway."

"The investigation?"

"No, justice—wait, did I get that right? Yes, here it is. 'It matters little.' 'No, justice.' Hmm, I said 'anyway,' I said 'it matters little anyway.' I think it's still okay though."

"I need to talk to my parents."

"I think you are supposed to talk to your killer, actually."

"I don't have a killer, detective."

"Nonsense. You better find one. Everyone has one and maybe if you would have found yours sooner—this wouldn't have happened, young lady."

"And if it didn't happen?"

"It matters little anyway. No, justice—crap. I think I got that wrong again."

DeDeAnne's bike scraped along the sidewalk the same way it always did when she picked it up carelessly, a tiny metallic red scratch left on the cement. The bike ticked and ticked the same way it always did when she walked it slowly. DeDeAnne passed all the houses she normally did and all the storefronts she normally did. She even stopped to coax the yapping dog behind the 'beware dog' fence like she always did.

"Do you think my killer is inside?" she asked the Pomeranian-Yorkie mix.

But it only yapped back and she imagined her days spent walking about town asking for her killer as if that is what young girls are supposed to do. What she needed was someone to work it out with her. Someone whom she trusted who could also keep a secret. Someone who would open their door if she showed up. And this someone, she began to realize, was most likely the one who was waiting for her unsuspecting body to end up in his or her hands. A teacher, a tutor. The grocery store clerk, the gas attendant. The priest, the town do-gooder. The mean guy, the bully kid. The silent one, the weirdo. Her parents, her neighbors, The Stranger, an authority. The no one. Everybody. It really could be anybody and it really was always everyone.

Before DeDeAnne went to the edge of the town to escape her killers and the haunting of her fated body, she decided to spend one last moment with her parents, and the family cat. At first, she worried she was indeed a ghost, as Time had left her home completely. Her mom sat at the kitchen table. Her dad at his desk. The cat at its empty bowl. If the wail was still here it was too loud to be heard. Its vibration became a vacuum. It was only when a small tuft of her mother's hair moved as DeDeAnne slid in next to her that she knew there was still time for her parents, there was still air, and there could still be a sound in the world.

"Not now," her mom said. The words so quiet it was almost as if they weren't said at all.

"I heard they found my body."

"Yes, your body, but not you."

"But I'm here now, Mom. Right here."

"I know, my hip aches. Like you could crawl back onto me. I think my body was built with you. You against my hip, against my shoulder. Your head in my crook. I'm still full of you—all my indentations are yours."

"They can be again. I'm right here, Mom."

"Did you find your killer?"

"Mom, I'm not dead."

"That matters little. We've been through so much already. When they found your—"

"I'm right here. Dad will see."

"Don't bother your father. He is not the same. We are not the same. It's just as they say, you know. The loss of a child. The horror of man. The evil in the world. It's just as they've said it would be. The stuff of nightmares. We should have warned you. Maybe we did. So many *should*s. So many ways we did things to keep you safe. The detective said we could lock up all the children and keep them under surveillance and maybe that is the thing the world should do—we should have done."

Her mother pulled DeDe's warm hand into her own. She kissed the tips and rubbed her forearm, she almost pulled her into her, like pulling at bed covers, like gathering warm laundry before dropping it onto the bed to be folded.

"There's always some child out there, DeDeAnne. In a field. In a basement. Brown girls like you in plastic trash bags in the river. We knew it happened, but never knew it could happen to us. We've only acceptance to do now. Moving on and one-day-at-a-time-ing and coping and your father and I will probably divorce and one of us might drink, or worse, and we'll lose the mortgage, of course, because we won't be able to work. First, the funeral though." Her mother sat up, wiped a tear. "DeDe, I don't think you should go to that. There's very little for you to do there. Go on now, you little dead thing. We've no use for your living now."

The family cat gave one last brush up against DeDeAnne's hand, darting away before she could touch her back. The soft padded steps of kitty paws made their way up to the family den to the father worn silent and should-ing above.

When the cars began lining up at the chapel, DeDe set her bike down on the grass and tried her best to stand out of the way. Many told her to get going and others said she was a lovely girl, but they've all their answers now. Others nodded and some ignored her completely. The neighborhood bully was the only one to stop to talk to her.

"You smell like the living," he jabbed at her and then shrugged and picked up a rock and threw it at nothing. "I don't know why I'm so mean," he said.

"I don't know why I'm dead," DeDeAnne said.

"You're not. Of course, you're not. But they tell me it matters little. Better to sort it out now, I guess. Have you been there yet?" He leaned close to her, the hand he placed on her shoulder was soft and gentle, barely the weight of a bird. "To your dump site? The crime scene? Your un-resting place?"

She shook her head.

He sighed and leaned even closer and kissed her cheek. "I just wish it were me."

"The stuff of nightmares," she said.

At the edge of the main road, at the edge of a road full of potholes, at the edge of the dirt road beyond that, at the edge of the field, at the edge of the woods, at the edge of the very town, DeDeAnne walked back and forth along a fence. The posts were too old and broken to touch, the thought of slivers frightened her. Who would care to pull them out? And the fence wire, though drooping and thin, seemed too dangerous a thing to cross. Something to be tangled in. Something to slow her down if she were running. Running for her life.

She thought to slump down and let the brush prick at her dress, thought to move no rock or stick, but only to sit and feel her way through a real death, a real last breath, a real permanent coldness to her. But there was a shuffle closing in. It started as if from everywhere, from every corner of every world. So known to us all, it took its time toward her. There was nothing but time for this sort of closing in. Nothing but its inevitable reach. She waited for it to come. For rough hands and a gentle voice or gentle hands and a rough voice. For it to be the last person she thought of and the first, for something in her—a nerve, a cellular knowledge, a fated code that said *Yes, this. I was built for only this.* The shuffle shrunk from all the space around her into one location, moved from her inner ear to her very real ears, gathered its speed. From the other side of a fence, a sigh-sob and the thwap-thwap of weeds hitting shins and knees.

A young girl from the neighboring town emerged.

"Can you see me?" she asked. "Am I alive?"

"I think so, but what do I know?" DeDeAnne said.

"They say I am dead. They say I've nothing but evidence to me anymore. Nothing but the will of the world. They say my body has been found and it's a 'nightmare of a world,'" the young girl said.

"The stuff of nightmares?" DeDe asked.

"No," the girl held the word long in her mouth. Then she said, a little brightly, a little hopeful, "The detective said, 'a nightmare of a world.'"

The two girls sat on either side of the fence, facing back toward their own towns, facing back toward the wails that emitted from them. That wail that said it's such a shame. That wail that said the world is going to hell. That wail that continued to ignore them, the living, and simply agreed the death of little girls was just another part of life and therefore another role to play.

"Well," said DeDeAnne, cheered enough to straighten her hair and smooth out her top. "Mine said 'stuff of nightmares.' So, at least there's that."

HERPES OF THE HEART

Three doctors confirmed I suffered from some sort of emotional herpes and they suggested I stop fucking everyone. No more *but I was bored, but he was cute, but she was cute, but they were bored and cute*; just close up that trap of myself. The thought of doing so flings me into the pursed lips of the pastor and I can't help wondering if his lips are as tight as his asshole. And if so, is there nothing to his endless drilling of me but perhaps a chance at undoing the "I've a daughter your age" look he thinks I haven't seen?

When done, he makes slow attempts at conversation and I watch the lights from cars on the highway hit the window of his hotel. Now and now. And now and not for a while again until the new now. It's past 3 a.m. My car is outside, but what's 3 a.m. when there's only waking up a few hours away.

"It's non-smoking," he says, and then something more about the road, the life, the lost. And I just nod and finish my smoke and start making the bed my very own. The thing about sleeping next to strangers is to pretend they aren't there when you're done. Otherwise, there are many night hours spent imagining them brushing their hand on your thigh as an invitation. Is it now? Do they want it now again? The same ways or new? Or perhaps when they want to hold you close, it's only to wring your neck. I don't know anyone that had a wrung neck, but it's what I think about along with the $178 from his wallet that I stole before he came out of the bathroom, before any of the naughty got started. I'd never done that before. I don't even know why I'm doing it now other than the fact I might have heart herpes and need some sort of follow-up appointment.

I finally decide that tomorrow I would see the same doctor I saw when I first turned eighteen. The one my mom took me to in order to get my insurance caught up with the just-that-day-turned-adult body. When he asked if I'd ever slept with anyone for money, my mom urged me to answer truthfully. I was a virgin then and it seemed impossible to me that they didn't see that right away. Half-a-dozen years since, though, everyone looks like they are taking it up the ass as much as possible. And loving it, of course.

The other three doctors heard me out and wrote some stuff down and then forgot everything I said while they instructed me into the stirrups and pushed and prodded and warned "A little cold now" and "Sharp pain here" and I immediately agreed that that was indeed the response I was having. But who really knows. Either way they weren't going to take care of my heart herpes. I figured the asshole that asked me—in front of my own mother—if I fuck for money would be the guy to tell me the truth and wouldn't a diagnosis solve it all? Wouldn't it explain why despite the pastor's sizable dick, what remains in my mind is the sag of his tighty whities under his flat ass? As if I never knew underwear could do that—could unshape a person. I fucked him anyway from boredom, because he looked sad, because it was all dead-beat drunks at the bar, and because he ordered me a pizza and pushed water on me after so very many drinks I had tossed back on my own.

That doctor was probably the same age as the pastor—probably suffering from the same sag of things meant to hug, hold, and accentuate. Not things I want to think about when he examines me, but it turns out the strip mall the doctor's office had been in looks abandoned now. No one bothered to strip off the fading, chipping wood pane exterior so fitting of the '70s. No one bothered to do more than scrape a little off the gold lettering. Someone did bother to put an Olive Garden on the other side of the parking lot and, well, they have free breadsticks.

You can't order a beer in this town before 11 a.m. at a restaurant and you can't have any cocktails made where families and kids can view it, which seems like exactly the reason all rapists should work at Olive Garden. I think about filling out an application myself, but then remember (I'm not a rapist and) I do actually have a job, even though I was on forced vacation since I've been working regularly at the same company since I was nineteen and someone happened to notice that I'm always there. Too much always there.

You'd think because I sleep with a strange preacher or because I stole money from him and because I have heart herpes that I work at a bar or in the only coffee shop in town—because we're in that type of town. But actually, I process reports and type close to 107 words a minute with only a 3% error rate. I never ask for instructions twice and no one notices me there because their work arrives regularly without any fuss or excuses. I'm also not necessarily pretty or hot, nor am I ugly or weird. Someone once told me there was nothing worse than a "weird" girl and I've taken that piece of bullshit with me everywhere. Don't be weird. Weird unfuckable, that is.

So instead, I just fall into the background of everything and yet end up on top of everyone. Wriggling or thrusting my fist or fingers up and up and never letting anyone do any of the work if I can keep it that way.

The second night at the same bar, my preacher—no—pastor friend, comes in and I can tell he's sorta peeking around looking for me and at first, I worry he's looking for his money and what would I say? I'm not really a thief or a criminal and I never was, not because I was scared or have some inner moral fiber, but it just wasn't on my radar of ways to fuck myself over. But there he is looking soft and it's as pathetic as you'd expect. He might even be trying to look a little more put together and when he walks over, I'm with my girlfriends and I make a little small talk. He shuffles and then gives up looking any certain way and just says something about me hanging with my mates and he'll talk to me later. I remind myself to check in on him in an hour or so in case there's nothing going on tonight.

My friends suspect nothing and never would and never have and I'm just that nice: a friendly friend that random people like to meet and everyone else likes to dump their shit upon because I'm too polite to ask them to shut up. I'm not a pushover though. I'm just ... without that depth that everyone around me seems to have, the one they throw themselves into and talk about endlessly. The one that makes an echo out of everything they say, eats the shadow of all they see. It's like they take everything ... personally. Always. And that's a hell of a lot of work.

I was hoping for a band to show up or some sort of spontaneous "let's get fucked" shot-mania to sweep into someone nearby me, but instead people are dwindling. Some are talking about very important things that will be left behind to ensure a good night's sleep ahead, or they are thinking about tomorrow and it's as if tomorrow is already here. The jukebox is playing the same eighteen songs I always play, carefully chosen not to piss off the bartender who has a button to push when he needs to skip a song or because they're all dicks. The thing is, I've only two more days of enforced vacation, and at some point, I need to clean, do laundry, visit my folks, and make my life a work-week life again. But for tonight, there's that god-awful preacher whose eye sockets are so much a vacuum that it's like his eyeballs have fallen too far into his head.

He's just so *old*.

I wish I could remember why he's no longer a pastor. Or if he was a minister. Or a preacher. I'm almost sure it's pastor. Wish I knew what makes one not that anymore. If you retire or take a leave or divorce it. Of course, asking means making all the signs of the face that say "Oh really?", "Oh fascinating," and "Wow." And I'm pretty sure my heart herpes has reached my face and now I've got emotional cold sores popping up, infecting my lips. That burn of the self all over the body. That tingle of disease. I'm afraid of shingles.

Pastor doesn't seem to care though and soon enough we are back at his could-be-anyplace hotel and I'm idly suggesting some anal, but for some reason am not as into it as usual and he's picked up on it and I think there's a layer of "are you sure you want to be here?" going on with him that makes me tired. The heart herpes has taken over my voice as well and I've nothing to say and I really mean it. Instead, I say something about the lights hitting the window and it sounds poetic and now he's in the layer of "crazy how casual sex can lead to poetry" or "ships in the night" or something. I say something about it being aliens and it is right about then that the fire alarm goes off.

The hotel is in that weird place between two close towns, so neither actually wants to claim it as their own. It's not even on the edge of something, which would be a great way to be. Like there's a cliff nearby, which maybe also means there's something to see. An overlook. But neither of those things happen in this part of the non-cities. Instead, it's like the gas station and hotel that everyone forgot about and the only ones that go there are traveling businesspeople and families living cheap on vacation. The men and women are shuffling out of the hotel and trying not to stare at one another in the hopes that no one else stares back at them. And I start muttering more about aliens and wasn't it odd that I mentioned aliens and now we are all standing around in this parking lot waiting for something to happen. But the sky is clear.

Pastor has reached the "seeing you in a new light" stage and maybe I am a weird girl and maybe that's the last thing anyone wants. Maybe I'm not young and carefree and fuck-shit-up girl, but instead I'm telling stories to myself and if he isn't careful he'll catch that too. Either way, I'm not ready to half-drunk drive back to my other-life apartment and I hope he's not done fucking this piece of meat and so I stop thinking about the aliens and instead ask him for real this time why he left his church.

There's no way others aren't listening in. The hotel manager and the hotel desk person, who both have new name tags, bustle about looking worried as shit, but a couple of staff in well-worn name tags are smoking near a parking lot lamppost and one is checking me out. I can tell he can hear me and the old pastor because he hasn't joined into their conversation and because he chuckled when I accepted the cigarette he offered but declined to stand and talk to him because I said I only smoke in non-smoking rooms, which wasn't what I meant to say and also sounds more interesting than it is. There's also a couple and then another single man standing out there and the couple has said all they are going to say for the rest of their marriage (or affair) and the single man is fake-looking at his phone.

Loud-like I say, "I just figure if you're going to give up trying to fuck me in the ass, you should tell me a little more about yourself and we can get to the bottom of this," and to this he says, "Okay, okay," and his hand is on my shoulder in that "quiet it up, missy" sorta way and I'm not weird anymore.

It's a long story, the pastor's. But the gist is he didn't give up his faith or lose it as much as he just got bored of it. And I guess this is a lot worse than anything else that could have happened to a pastor. He isn't saying as much, but when he's talking about other people of faith that have lost their way, I can see a longing in his eyes, like that feeling I get when I want to be in someone else's song. Losing faith probably means it's right where one left it. And the pastor agrees when I tell him this with another look of "strangers … night … poetic." At least someone who lost their faith can take those steps back to it. They can see where and why they put it down and maybe why it was obscured for so long.

But it seemed to me that this pastor has carried his with him still. And it's just that it's like an ID card or a penny lost in a fold. It's just there and he has had no use to pull it out again, which makes me think of his dick and whether or not he'd kept that hidden until last night too. I can't remember what he sells on the road, so it must not be that great. Or maybe he just checks up on certain businesses. I don't know if people sell things on the road anymore actually and I'm about ready to ask him this, but he's staring off at the mountains and the alarm has ended and people are shuffling back in.

And though no one is asking, I suddenly feel like I want to explain to my co-middle-of-nothing-sleepers it's not that I actually feel diseased. It's just that something attached to me during a sexual bout a couple weeks ago and it hasn't lifted. It keeps spreading everywhere I go. And it's not curable, so it's become a part of me now and I'm fearful of outbreaks. There's a spell of spreading and what it means to spread oneself open and to leave parts of oneself with another and it's taken up space in my cells.

I'd been chained to a bed for over twenty minutes, which probably doesn't seem long unless you are the one chained there. When I say chained, I mean chained. Not fuzzy or even regular handcuffs. Not silky, soft rope. I mean, this dude liked it rough. And I was into that. Like *into* it so that I couldn't even feel me anymore. And I won't say we were animals, but we certainly weren't human and when I pulled my arm during a particularly loud howl and he simultaneously yanked at me and then something wonky happened where the bed frame broke, my wrist gave like the crush of melting snow. You know when it still looks crunchy on top, but underneath it's all turning into a slush and you step on it and are surprised by how quickly it just gives way? It was totally like that. Not a break, but a collapse of the thought of bone.

And then there was a lot of madness as the dude worried about me and cops and lawyers and doctors and back to me. And other such nonsense as if I couldn't just drive myself to the ER if I really needed to. I eventually told him my girlfriend would be mad if I didn't call her if I was taken to the hospital and that she would meet me there and he should not talk to me again unless we are going to finish what we started. He never asked what my girlfriend would say about my cheating on her because like most men if you mention girlfriend, they can only think we are two lipstick lesbians super soft and easy with one another and that the only fights we have are ones with pillows. It's a good way to get out of any other questions though. And because sometimes it's true I have a girlfriend, though she never sticks around for long.

Anyway, my wrist had hurt like hell and it was a real bother cleaning up after myself and maybe even though it was days and days or weeks ago and no longer did I need that sling, but just a bit of a bandage when I was home or at work, maybe this is why I was forced to take a vacation. Someone noticed I might be a person that should be in pain instead of stifling my cursing while typing and someone else said something about how hard they worked me and no one wanted to be accused of anything, especially the dude that did this to me who was also my boss's brother. I dunno. Maybe my boss knew, maybe he didn't. The thing is they said I should take a week or two off and go somewhere and see something or just rest. *Just rest.* And it was then that I began to recognize the heart herpes I had.

Because no matter whom I slid into body with after that, I always felt like I was taking something and giving something back beyond the pleasure. Like there was another type of exchange at work and if I could only figure out what it was, then maybe I'd have a shot at curing it. I'm not saying I don't want to fall in love or have a monogamous relationship, but damn shouldn't we all be able to have the safest of sex in which we don't leave with a single memory of it or can at least carve the memory out of the other before wiping up and shutting the door behind us? Isn't that what prostitution is for? And damn that old gross doctor for making me feel like it could have been a bad profession for me. Money for sex. Straight across. Can you imagine the end of all the small talk and the morning light goodbyes? And the running into the fucker again on the next night in the same bar and the way he sorta loitered around me trying to talk or trying to see me when I was just the background noise of the girls around me? And I only went to his hotel with him again so I wouldn't have to ask myself why I went there in the first place.

The point is, here's a worthless piece of shit who has faith but won't even use it and here I am suffering from the realization that when one ties you up with real chains (and knocks you around a bit as you desire and consent to and in the best ways all the while stimulating your genitals with once-frozen glass dildos and various foodstuffs to be licked off), you are engaging in something called trust—maybe not trust of the mind and certainly not trust of the heart but a body contract that both of you sign with each moan and quick-like-a-needle intake of breath. It's a terrible feeling to not be able to just dissolve one's fuckmeat like angler fish do or to at least release them from their contract without a single moment of the future sinking it. If we could make ourselves forget certain things, our body memory would sing its elation and I could watch *Battlestar Galactica* with the same fascination when I saw it the first time.

But the pastor was leaving in the morning and would most likely never be in this city again and if he would be, I probably wouldn't be because after a week off of work, it's pretty obvious I'm too fucking smart for that job and for this tiny town. Plus, I've plenty of family and really great friends living all over the country and all of them have invited me out to stay on their couch while I look for a job and a new place and they say "potential" to me a lot. The reality is I'd never see him again and probably forget his face.

But he'd still think of me and remember me and a part of me was in his blood the same way the heart herpes was in mine. The same way I was always feeling maybe maybe maybe I really do like the boss's brother because he has a wide, good smile and puts an open palm on my arm when he asks me questions and he's funny as fuck and we like all the same music and I've told him some things about my family and opened up about real life things. And he never cared to hear what I've done with other men or women, the way so many of the people I meet lean in close and ask to feel the same heat I am describing when I fuck strangers in elevators or in that construction zone that also happened to be in the center of several hotel towers at the heart of this stupid city.

The ex-pastor was leaving in the morning, but also never really leaving either and when we climbed back into bed and he paused a second as if to maybe ask me something or to let me know he sees me—really sees me as a person, I quickly asked him if he ever thought someone could be released from his or her heart. And obviously he thought I was being poetic again and not talking about contracting an incurable, life-long contagion of emotion. And he started in about his church and his family and how easily people can feel redemption if they seek it.

It's then that I confess I could show him redemption if he lets me grab some chains from my car and if he's ready for that pinched ass-hole of his to make some amends with itself. And has he seen his skin raw with small red beads from a good thirty-five minutes of spanking and whipping and he should start by getting on his knees. And he nods and says God forgive me and when I worry for half a second that I might end up actually hurting him because what I really want is to wipe his memory away while also undoing whatever lovesick I contracted from my boss's totally doable and nice guy brother, I decide that if this pathetic old pastor and this weird heart-girl are going to exchange anything tonight, it better start with a safeword.

BY THE CONTENTS OF HER . . .

PURSE

Three lip glosses. Two unused, department store. One well-used, grocery-store quality. Looks like clay with brushed marks in it from her lips. She needs to use a balm more. I've told her so. The "Red and Rad" and "Pink Fusion" ones from Macy's are from me. "Red and Rad," never opened.

Receipts. Cash mostly. Change for twenties. Once a card—last four digits, I don't recognize. Maybe it's from a gift card. Maybe her father's credit card.

Candy wrappers. Assorted.

A sleek and small address book. It's cute. Metallic cover that clasps, sprawling cherry blossoms along the front and back. Thin white-white rectangular papers held within it. The lines for names and addresses blank. Some pages ripped out. Maybe she uses it as a note pad.

All-Natural Blotting Paper for Sensitive Skin. Expensive.

GRADES

A-/B+ average. I don't know if she needs a scare, a shot of coffee, or a firm but tender hand on her shoulder. Maybe a tour to the college of her choice. I don't know what she needs to leave behind that B+. But she's always been like that. Even as a child, she'd hedge herself in as if she didn't want anyone to see the best of her. As if asking for her to accept her potential was a crime. Like we were pushing her too hard to emerge from a cocoon. Her wings not sturdy-formed, but soupy and slow. But honestly, what was she doing in there? Lagging. She doesn't get her shoes all the way on before she's stuck negotiating with the mirror by the front door and her father honking outside.

"She needs her own car," he says.

"A timebomb," I say.

TEARS

She wasn't much of a crier when she was young and watching her tears well reminds me that they are precious things we won't see again. She has golden hair, the way everyone told me I had golden hair. Her sobbing-self pressed against mine, her hair smells of apricot and cream. The ends need trimming.

"Let's get some makeup and a haircut? Croissant and espresso? My treat."

She sniffs and then pushes off me like a swimmer pushing off into a backstroke. I check my shirt for any shiny remnants of her fluids.

"I don't want to," she says. Heads back to that room of hers. Stereo hammering.

NORTH FACE BACKPACK

Rose—the tag boasts. But it's a bubblegum rose. The rose of a tween. Rose candy. It was a practical purchase, but the rose color allows for a little flair. She wanted a blue-black one. However, the only one they had was scuffed and she set it down, staring at the price tag, at me, at the sales assistant, and back at the bag. She took a breath and nodded at the rose one in my hand. Walked away. The same way she walked away from the dessert table at her grandmother's eightieth birthday party. The same way she walked away from her father and I after another failed attempt at trying to get out of dance class. Resigned.

I reach to pull the backpack out of the giant plastic bag it is in. To pull off the evidence tag on the plastic bag and let some air into that stale world. The rest of the contents lay out on the kitchen table. More plastic bags. More tags.

"Do either of you recognize any of this?"

DIARY

She has none.

BODY

The hair, if washed, might be the same. Might move the same. Might be the same sort of heaviness that was hers. But the arms don't seem right. Too toned. If muscle was something those arms could flex. If the skin wasn't so gray and made of crude rubber. And the hips too narrow. And the legs, something about them. Well, one of them. The other takes up a space under the sheet, but not the one you'd expect to see. That side of her body and most of her face as well, a mangle of flesh under the sheet.

"It's not Joy," my husband says. "She has no hands."

"It's not her," I say. "Not enough . . . her."

It's someone's girl though. This one with that tight body and with toes as though she didn't walk a lot. Manicured, soft, slender. She didn't run, dance, swim. Not like our girl.

"She was always busy," I tell the detective. I sign a form that says we were there. It goes into a file with all the others. Time measured by paper. "You know, she's . . . involved. Active. She's going to college."

ALERT

Her father showed me a picture of her from her Facebook page. The angle taken from above. Her right cheek facing out, her head cocked. Closed-mouth smile, a little too much chin. Eyebrows pulled up, like she's surprised-happy. Part of her right arm showing, the one she uses to hold the camera.

"No."

The alert shows her at her grandmother's birthday bash. A burgundy top that brings out the dark flecks in her light brown eyes. Her arm around Connie, Constance, my mother. Her smile—open, big teeth. The words "Abducted on 5/2/13" almost go unnoticed.

She's such a pretty girl. They say, "She was always such a pretty girl."

WINDOW

From the loose garden by the fence (the one I've always told Mitch to rip out and cover with grass) her window can be seen, only partially covered by the chokeberry tree. Maybe she moved back and forth from her desk to her bed. Maybe she got dressed as the sun emerged. The light rose and orange colors bouncing off her window would blind the view of the yard below from her. At the right angle, someone could see everything. If she laid her clothes out, the way I laid them out for her when she was young, she'd take a few seconds to look over the outfit. Her back would be to the window. Her bra straps and band flashing a deep turquoise or purple or black (no, nude—she always wore nude) at whomever might be watching her from below.

Though she probably didn't smooth out her skirt and blouse on the bed. Didn't unroll her tights and stream them across both top and bottom. Didn't hold her shoes up next to the outfit, looking for oddities or clashing.

No. She burrowed into her closet for a certain top. Pulled clumped and wrinkled jeans from a pile on a desk chair. Shoes and socks on her way out the door. A last check at the mirror in the foyer to make sure her hair was less tangled than before.

"Someone could have watched her getting ready from the yard," I say.

Her father might not hear me. He stares at the front door. "I'm sorry. What was that?" he asks the detective before he avoids looking at me.

SCREAMS

You'd think she was raised in a barn. As if life were a walk in the park. Well, what can you expect from a hog but a grunt? Why buy the . . .

Things her grandmother Connie would say if she were still here. If either of them were still here. If Connie could remember the last match between Joy and I, she'd recognize her hand in mine, in that slap I delivered. Recognize the "How dare you talk to me like that!" glaring eye. The chin moving up and away from my chest, my body, my stalk and instead reaching for the tops of something. As if I could raise my head above hers, though she had grown to my height. That slap was the only height and weight I had left for her. Full hand. Full swing. Full flush of Joy's face.

"Why don't you trust me? Why don't you believe in me?" Joy raises her hand to her face. Holds her face back together while her body twitches and shudders.

Why buy the cow when you can get the milk for free?

"I'm not like that," she said. Took that slap that I sent to her face and threw it back onto the marble counter. The "Fuck You" scream filled the house. Ended all other possible ends. She held her own, but only another few seconds before heading up stairs.

Calm. Quiet. Awake. I followed closely behind her.

REPORT

Her father's "But I thought you said" kept nothing at bay. His "Wait, you said" and "What about" and "This doesn't make any sense" were all phrases that crumbled before they hit the ground. Nothing stuck.

They were wrong. He was wrong. The initial reports were wrong.

"It's a missing persons case now."

A runaway.

They'll still follow leads, but they are soft now. Not the thick and black arrows on a dry erase board. Not the series of question marks across the brow. Not the steady writing of every note and statement and then say it again. Describe it again. "Again, Mrs. Randell, the last time you spoke to her, she . . ."

She did not tell her own mother to "Fuck off." She did not slam her hand down on the counter. She did not turn away from me—not me—and head up to her room as if I had no business of following her there.

Soft leads. A nod to check the local teen hangouts. Check the bus schedules. Send around that humiliating Facebook post asking for strangers to look out for her. Asking some pervert to wait for her to pass his house. She, too dumb a thing to think the world had moments waiting for her. Moments that she didn't have to build herself by pushing all the math into the right place. Take the opportunity. Take the best scores. Take it and don't stop and make your own future. Or he'll take it for you.

ANNIVERSARY

Her father fields the calls. The flowers. The emails. He hires a private investigator. He takes time off work. He postpones birthdays, Christmas, St. Lucia, and promotions. When the police are done in her room, he puts everything back in its place. Unread, unopened. Sometimes he leaves something in there: a glass of water, flowers, or a book. The new center of our house is her room. Everything pulls toward it. Everything falls into it. There is no time, but the time that keeps the room together. When the Honda advert he taped to her bedroom door falls down, I don't throw it away. I set it on the hallway table next to her door. Wait for him to tack it on there again. A promise for securing her freedom. It'd come with GPS.

CONCEPTION

If the eggs in me felt full.

If they drove me here or there.

If her father's embrace didn't have a hint of sadness, didn't wane.

If so many days weren't between our encounters.

If the DNA of us every time added up in the same way.

If seventeen years didn't settle into our bodies and make so many demands.

If there were the slightest chance we could make you again, I think your father wouldn't hesitate.

FLEETING REFLECTION

On cold mornings, the kind that never seem to warm up and come from a night of piling on blankets and socks and moving to the couch to flip through channels waiting for something boring enough to lull me to sleep, I would have said something—anything, any "Your father won't be okay with this" or "Please at least take some money," anything—other than my quiet while I had pretended to sleep.

By the contents of her fleeting reflection in the foyer mirror, she seemed steady. She keyed the code—the one I said I un-set because I opened the door when "I thought I heard something outside, detective . . . near the fence in that patch of useless garden that looks up into her window." She opened the door with a soft, slow tug. She took a big breath, like she was setting up an air supply in some black hole of her lungs. I heard the door close with a *pfft*. Not the slam like the slam of her hand on the counter. Not the screech of her voice. Not the sharpness of that final "Fuck you." But like a little bubble caught in the air about to pop with no one to hear it.

She closed the door like how I closed the door behind her every school day, sending her off to her father's waiting car. My "Don't forget" and "I don't want to hear it again" and "Just sign up and see" and "Who knows, just get yourself in and then find out" and "I just want the best for you" filling the pockets of air behind her. I'd close that door, sending her off to a future ahead. And me, I'd turn around to face the house that I built as a launching pad for her. A house that hours later would take her in again and breathe her out. Except not this one time. That night: the sting of my hand still on her face, her curse to me still echoing, the story of her emptying as I pretended not to see her reflection in the entryway. She closed the door how she'd never let it close before. Closed for good. My girl.

SURVIVOR'S GUIDE

It's all under the wrapping paper. In the downstairs guest room closet. Somewhere Elisse's husband would never find it, because unlike Elisse, he could never get the wrapping paper to surrender to the corners of any box with that willing crease and easy smoothing out of surfaces that Elisse seemed to charm from the paper. He'd left that nonsense up to her and left the rolls of wrapping paper in the downstairs guest room closet: pillars of her domain. He didn't know the paper was camouflage, hiding the canisters of beans and flour and sugar. At first, there was enough room in the corner of the closet, but then Elisse had to remove the spare sheets and comforter and two baby quilts from too many years ago. Had to find some sort of space-age technology that is only sold in the late-late-night-right-before-it-turns-early-morning hour. She took a vacuum to the space bag full of sheets and blankets and sucked the air out of the bag. The attachment wouldn't hold because she didn't (But wait! For only five dollars more!) order the one from the commercial and, instead, used her own attachment from the handheld vac. But, obviously, it still got the job done. The baby quilts she lied about giving to a donation center and the sheets and blanket for guests that never arrived had the air sucked out around them. They collapsed to nearly an inch thick. A flattened life. Pushed under the always-made guest bed.

The space bags freed up room for the other goods. The flashlights and, oh yes, the WaterBob Emergency Drinking Water Bathtub Storage device. Elisse's husband had pointed it out at Home Depot and walked away chuckling (not out loud, but like he does—in his chest). Sure enough, she went back the next day and grabbed up two (okay, maybe four) and kept them stored behind the guns. Yes, the guns. She would never be able to explain this part to him. All the years of his family buying guns, and she saying, "Never in this house," and admitting it wasn't about the gun itself but the accidents around them. And never admitting she didn't want something so close to her that could end it all right then. Pills might afford some time for her to change her mind. Razors not so much, which is why she forbade them as well (except the dozen or so in the emergency supply kit, tsk). And who would hang themselves? Of course, now we can all think of at least three people who did. It's sad like that. Saying out loud, "No one would do such a thing—but oh, that poor girl did," and "Him." That's the him that we shake our heads about, and heartsunk but all the while knowing it is cliché, we say, "But why? Why?! So much to live for. What a shame!" when we put his book down. No, Elisse's first option was always the pills. But the gun seemed too easy and efficient and, so, she said politely and with as much respect as she could for very responsible types that do keep their guns in safe places and haven't rattled off the location of said safe place to neighbor kids and the family's trouble-maker cousin, she said, "No. Not now. No gun in the house."

But Now came when she could not find a guide to a survivor's kit without a gun listed among essential materials. All mid-morning internet reading and clicking at 24-Hour, 72-Hour, 7-Day, 1-Month, 1-Year survivor kit pages had bulleted or, at least, noted guns. Some with "Go get one! Today!" hyperlinked to gunsamerica.com. Rabbit hole link, she always called it. So, she gave in to the handy 11-in-1 Survivor Tool and the razors and other blunt objects like the DeWalt Heavy Duty

Flashlight and that damn new baseball bat (instead of asking the many friends and family that are sure to have one forgotten in the garage). Yes, she bought a bat made of northern white ash and kept it snug in the closet. If it is good enough for the Major Leagues . . . And then, finally, the guns.

We can't begin to imagine how she managed to buy them. The paperwork and costs aside, she had to have had a lot of questions, amateur ones or "Questions to Ask" printed out from the "Buy A Gun" page of How.com. And, of course, the ending up with a half-dozen options (at least) and hoping to get them down to three, but not wanting to tell the clerk so. Elisse probably couldn't imagine how it happened either, even though she was there. That's how these things go sometimes, the body and mind work and the muscles move and the throat constricts and relaxes. Air and sound come out and then one comes home with a First Alert Five Live Bolts and 6mm Recessed Door Gun Safe and a .22. Then a 9 mm. And a .45. And her self, made of memories and wants and silly nostalgia for pumpkin-flavored and -scented everything during the fall, had left her. Elisse—a vapor in the wake of the moving, doing, an acting body that needs a gun.

What Elisse's husband wouldn't understand after finding the guns is the amount of Stride gum, blood pressure meds, and copies of Uncle Remus stories piled up between the gun safe and the canisters of food. His favorite gum. His type of medication in bottles of various dosages, each with a stranger's name on it. His most remembered tales read to him by his racist-in-the-way-most-older-generations-were-racist mother. But she included several editions of the book as if she didn't know which was the one he remembered; Elisse was thoughtful like that.

But nothing could prepare him for the schematics he found in a softened-to-a-manila-fuzz, worn envelope from the Loss Mitigation Department of their mortgage company on her desk. It had been there many months. Old refinance paperwork, he assumed. Instead: an 8x8 underground bunker. And a 10x10 one. Print-outs from a "Design Your Own Bunker" site. He'd liked to have found the print-outs for the next size up bunker schematics, but instead only her hand-drawn schematics were left. He had to hold that notepad paper with an entire underground bunker-home drawn on it up to his face real closely to read each detail. It had space for a 37" flat screen TV and a cubby craft corner. *What the hell, Elisse?*

Many would say she had so many tragedies in her life. They'd bumble around the mortuary viewing room and say to one another, "Elisse had so many tragedies in her life. Poor thing." Her father's "losing battle with cancer" (a morbid mantra of sorts) was too much after losing her mother so unexpectedly. And her frail Matty, poor Elisse, the loss of a child is unnatural. Or "It's unnatural to outlive one's own child," many said. The neighbor Maudell, who always got every saying wrong, would say "It's unnatural to outgrow one's own child." And we would not correct her at a time like this and no one would walk away and feel the neck sag and the eyes roll up the way one does when stuck in a small room with Maudell, whose continual usage of "suppose to be" instead of "supposed to be" spun our blood, especially when she'd next remind us the word was always "world-wind," not "whirlwind." That Maudell, smelling of generic dried peanut butter and forcing each of Elisse's distant relatives into her arms to nestle in the soft folds of her neck and that massive bosom.

Some would even say Elisse's receptionist job at the vet was too much for her—all those unhappy pets. Really? We'd nudge each other and squeeze one another's hand. Sink a snort or laugh back into the empty belly. Thinking of which restaurant we'd eat at afterwards and some errand to run and how the cadence of rising voices about Elisse's life of tragedy was a selfish type of mourning. How under that whir was still the stone-gut "What The Fuck, Elisse?" sensation that kept us from imagining that she wasn't just around the corner, ready to answer questions or close to sending another text about her latest failed baking attempt. No, no one would talk about how bad of a baker she was, though it seems it should be added to the tragedies in her life because she couldn't get enough banana or zucchini bread. Or donut holes ("which are fewer calories than actual donuts," she would say. Har har, Elisse.)

This life of tragedy wouldn't give an excuse for the drunk driver that hit her, of course. We don't excuse them at all. We can't. The same way we don't talk about rapes in prison. What's to say? But somehow the idea that tragedy was always welling up around Elisse would make the details of the accident fold up nicely. The way I dropped the phone when I got the call—not because I was shaken up but because I had been pulling clods of snow from my Shih Tzu's belly and my hand was cramped and numb—and the finding of the survival kit and guns and Stride gum and underground home-bunker plans all making sense. Elisse's tragic death and her tragic life and her attempts to stave off tragedy with items secured in a 2x6-foot closet. And the tiny fury that came when her pine coffin, on its way into the earth, escaped a strap, and scuffed a bit against the concrete burial vault—all part of God's plan. Her new coffin with a thick meaty scratch near where Elisse's head must be. And her husband, in a voice he hadn't used when he asked us to pick out her burial clothes or when he called caterers, florists, and the credit card companies, but with a higher voice, the kind of a sleeping child asking a question to anyone who might pretend to have an answer, said as the coffin swayed back to a stillness, "Oh. Is she alright in there?"

THE AGE OF PLASTIC

The two sides of the plastic bags rubbing against one another, my fingers jutting in and out between them. I wish I had latex gloves on. Wish my skin was empty of flaw and boasted a rubber sheen. Wish I embraced my thermoset life—always threatening to shrink, melt, shrivel under pressure. That sickly smug smell of me. "Early inflatable creations were made of dried animal bladder," I almost say aloud to Neil as he pumps away on top of me.

"She didn't know she was a blow-up doll."
"Did you tell her?"
"I—"

I try to loosen my hips. Make them rise and fall with the gravitational pull of the bed in this made-to-look three-star hotel room. I can't keep from wanting to pull him further inside me. But must concentrate on the bags on the side of the bed, allow my arm to stay draped down to them. My fingers gliding the sides of the plastic bag against one another. It's not enough. The plastic is too thin. Too boring. Too much the feel of too many plastic bags from pharmacies and grocery stores along I-70. They held toothbrushes, Tums, some chocolates, cheap socks. Forgotten things. Outdone things. Too many roads things.

"Fine. I had a dream," Neil says. "There was a blow-up doll."

I'm tempted to use the grocery bag to wipe myself off. Watch the glob of semen make its way across the blue lettering on the bag. Dip into the creases. Smell the moment when the two materials meet. The hint of a chlorine-like scent from him and that unashamed, unassuming smell of plastic. Neil is worried, but not about plastic. About the nine hours in the car and my refusal to stop earlier. He thinks I'm overdoing it and feels guilty for responding to my attempts to arouse him. "We should have flown," he wants to say. But only kicks the plastic bags out of his way as he heads toward the shower. He loves me.

"She didn't know. She thought she was real."

At the Dollar Deals in Tulsa, the tablecloths look more textured than I'd want. A crisscross pattern on that obnoxious blue that only exists in dollar store items. Not appealing. But the shower curtains . . . a thickness worth exploring. Though the size of it, the excuses for keeping it near the bed, would it bend and fold in my hands? Neil tells me the last time he had dollar store candy the top of his mouth turned bumpy and raw. We'll have to go to the grocery store for the rest. He doesn't remember my excuse for coming here. "Why are you looking at shower curtains?"

"Did you tell her?"

The Dollar Deals latex gloves are surprising. A purple a thirteen-year-old would love. A purple that provides a kick to neutral or copper and black IKEA kitchens across the U.S. This purple at my fingertips. They stick together too much. A tiny moment of sliding before they halt and bunch. Stubborn. Or just dry. My hand is under the pillow in front of me, the glove underneath it. I can only feel it slide now and again, never a rhythm. Unsure how to suggest I put it on, I slid it under the pillow as Neil undressed. The glove a failure, like all dollar store items end up being. Instead, I make my mouth look like an "O"—look at me: I'm surprised. I'm ready. I don't know I'm both. Behind me, Neil puts a hand on the center of my back, keeps his other holding onto my hips. We are not faced towards the mirror. Maybe next time he can see my face. This perfect "O" threatening to collapse into the biting of lips and soft, but full pleas.

"It was just a dream."

I'm very fond of Halloween; Neil knows this. It is no mystery for me to be lingering in the costume aisles even at a grocery store. The pharmacist is taking longer than most. It's Amarillo, the middle of somewhere to somewhere. Neil is patient. He's not worried even though we only made five hours of road since Tulsa, one less than the day before. He's starting to fall into our time, this journey, this last of something. The demand of just-in-case sex. He stands by the pharmacy, legs apart, rocking on his heels. Checking his phone for worlds outside of ours. It's normal for me to wander aisles. To touch a can of soup and continue forward as if my arm is attached straight and true. My hand falls behind as my body moves forward and I end up lightly touching each can of soup from one end of the aisle to the other. No one will come stop me. If they do, we'll say I'm waiting for my meds. We're headed to Sunstone Treatment Center. It's one of the best in the nation. The stock people and cashiers will nod and tuck their lips as if to smile. "Will you die?" they want to ask. Plastic gloves for a witch costume. It's so close to Halloween, I'll say. It's so close. Let's. I'll wear the gloves and keep the plastic grocery bag nearby. We've only ten or so hours until Phoenix, though Neil insists we take it slow. Stay in Amarillo and in Albuquerque. I need my rest, "especially with these nights of yours." He winks.

"No one wanted to tell her. She thought she was real."

Neil is sly and playful and alert. The gloves and the pointy hat threaten to fall off my bouncing head. We've moved to the floor. It feels new to him—not me on top, but the floor and the get-up. He nixed the crooked green witch nose. When I took it off and dropped it onto the floor, I feigned imbalance. Had to reposition quickly. He said, "You okay? We can stop." My left hand landed on the plastic bag from the store. The skin of my hand now so many small moments away from the carpeted floor. Between the two: a slipping of self. The witch gloves move like ice. A little slick from his sweat. The plastic underneath resisting and giving, resisting and giving. At the height of us, I move my hand to the side of the bed to steady myself. The bag sleek and giving against my palm.

"I just knew. The way you know in dreams."

A woman in a sex shop is always aware of how many people are looking at her. It might be a glimpse and sometimes a longer peek. And then there are the weirdos trying to make eye contact. It's true everywhere, even at the Walmart of sex shops, Castle Megastore of Albuquerque. I smile at Neil. Don't walk towards him and grab his hand though. Just a good long smile. He's in the fuzzy handcuffs and taste-great condoms section. The sensuous massage, first time, and bachelorette gift section. He likes the prices there. I'm sizing up the 16" hot pink two-sided dildo. The Passion Pink Double Dong from Masterplay Exotic Toys. Only because it's so close to Cindy. The inflatable, ready-when-you-are Cindy. She floats above the metal wall-racks boasting a buffet of dildos in various colors, sizes, and shapes—all housed in their tight, hard plastic packaging. The strings holding Cindy up are only visible if I press up against the wall closely and fancy a look behind her. I pretend I'm inspecting the grooves and veins of the Double Dong before looking up at her. Our ever-ready angel. From the ceiling to her neck, from the wall to her waist, fishing line. The glint of shine when the light catches it right. Her eyes are the same blue of Dollar Deals plastic dinnerware and party streamers. But she's not cheap. She's an-atomically "correct"—not "similar" as the fleshlights boast. And she doesn't look like she'll burst if left in the sun.

"Like your dream," I point up at Cindy when Neil comes closer.

"Huh?"

"Your dream of the plastic sex doll that thought she was real."

"I forgot about that," he says, staring at the Passion Pink Double Dong.

"It felt like sex with plastic, I guess. It was just a dream."

Neil has his head against my bare shoulder. His arms are wrapped around and under me. The back of my head—up near the crown—is on the pillow, neck arched. I think I could almost see the hideous portrait of dull moody desert that hangs above the hotel bed. If I could just arch my back further, if my neck was a synthetic play of molding. But Neil's weight keeps me from doing so. And I don't settle my head back into a comfortable position for fear of removing the safe spot he has found against my chest. "Sorry," he says. "This isn't such a bad idea, I guess." The hours of driving, the frequent stops, the lingering on park benches and making up stories about fellow road warriors. The father swearing at his giggling children. The woman with a license plate from across the country, driving in a dress and heels. And the lone ones, leaving bits of themselves along the open road. Some with a schedule coding their every move. Checking their phones constantly. "It's going to be fine. Really," he says.

I think he is ready to try again.

The kisses, those long familiar movements of tongue and lips. Sixteen years of this, he and I. He begins holding the end of them longer. *Don't move away. Let it start here, now*, I tell myself. My lips once pink. Once full. Imagine them red and set. I move my head to the side as he leaves kisses down my neck. The large "O" of my mouth forms. *Hold it. Don't let it go.* My skin once a layer of memory. Capturing the sensation of wind along it. Sites of scratchy, of something below the surface itchy and dry. The hair—years told. It can be a world made flat now. A new durable type of thinness. Unsurprising. Predictable. Certainly less prone to wear itself out every moment. My torso, a waiting thing. My arms and legs, no longer the keepers of doing. The limbs of things happening. The holding, handling, reaching, steadying, one-leg-before-the-other. The endless stepping towards no-one-knows. Another some hours from Sunstone Treatment, let all of it and, even this, happen to her. A Cindy-me with string showing only when you look closely enough. I bump the things around me so lightly, you only imagine I had moved. This body a resistance, but only full of your stale air. A world of empty, held by fine-tuned synthetic polymer and a dream. *Let's get used to this.*

"No one wanted to tell her she was a blow-up doll. She thought she was real."

WHITEBARK WOMAN

That's her singing. She sings from the mountains and on the windy days more so than others. She lights a fire now and then, but mostly she sings and watches and sways. The last group of hikers said they felt the mountain move, and I said it was my Netta. She sings the language of the mountains and the mountain moves with her. The hikers give me orange juice and some quarters. They tell me to sit right here.

"Sit right there and we'll find some help."

They don't know I have found help in the mountain song of my Netta. She wasn't always a song, but she's taken the mountain by surprise, I think. Some say she would take it over eventually. "Her story would be everywhere," they had said and told me to hush it down and hold to her picture instead. But my Netta took the mountain by surprise. She is a lush girl of fourteen and though she no longer ages, she has room in her to grow. She began as a simple voice along the paths. *Stay to the right. Hug to the rock.* She warns, *Sit under the dead trees,* even though the live ones seem to give more shelter. But some of those living trees are liars and only grow on the tiring of travelers. Your dreams and memories whisper to the trees and they eat them up. *Stay true to my song,* my Netta warned. But no one listened and three or five now have fallen along the rocks to meet the ground in a blow.

My Netta, she sings the mountains higher, I tell people. She lived in the dying Whitebark trees and under the stars. And on the rain-days and the storms and the snows, she huddled with smaller creatures into their furs and parts of her scampered out every few days to find a little more food. She lived in the ants, even then, and built worlds of walking under the ground and into the living things around her. She built walkways in the air and traveled them in her breath and voice. They say my Netta could be living anywhere, and they are right. She lives in the rivers.

My Netta, she will tell you all when she will be here. She is coming back, after all. She cannot live there forever, only a girl of eternal fourteen. She does not come yet because she does not desire to do so. Though some say she hasn't the path home or the feet or legs for walking it. They do not know her like I do.

When Netta was thirteen, she was a champion of letters made into words and she knew every story of the world. When she was twelve, she could slump into her chair long enough to become invisible and this was another secret power. When eleven, my Netta saw the future and she said to me, "You need help." My Netta at ten was a fully formed being, though she didn't wear it. She had all her grown-up moves in her and she kept them quiet for as long as she could. My Netta has a way with ways. She susses them out and coaxes and asks politely. My Netta at four was polite and at five she wouldn't scare, but waited for her punishments and rewards.

My Netta will bring her justice to this town as well. All those that said I hush it up in the summer times when folks around the world stretched out on our greens and blues, they will be punished. The smaller ones (now grown) who said "I believe you, Rose. I believe you" will be rewarded with Netta's careful know-hows.

In the earliest moments of this mountain, before it jutted itself out from the ground, before it told the ground it needed to believe in things higher and better, and, most importantly, it needed space to grow all the things it knew out and into the branches and animal kinds—before all of that, the ground didn't know of Netta. It didn't know what it was like to not want to be so flat and careful. But the mountain knew, the way my Netta knew and when they met at the top of themselves, they knew they couldn't just come right back home.

The dinner uncooked in packages in the pantry. The bathroom light still flickering. Me, a thing of worms still. Back then, a thing of worms and the liquids to keep them wriggling and moving these bones and flesh around. Some said she had nothing to come home to. Some said, "No wonder." Those ones say she went up, up, and away. But it is all a wonder, my Netta. They did not know my Netta loved me and would never leave. And though she may have been quiet the first decade or so on the mountain, reports of her came in. A woman in the Whitebark pines. She tended to stay near them. Sometimes leaning in so close that she mistook herself for the curves and bend of the tree's trunk. She learned to sway her arms about and her hair grew into knots. The reports of hikers finding a way back down the mountain and never finding it again. A child lost in the meadow, only to return three days later singing a song only my Netta would sing. My Netta stays close to the ones she can save.

IN THIS DREAM OF WAKING, A WEAVER

None of Klea's limbs or bones answered her. She lay like a stone being, demanding her spine to obey. The ceiling, a new coldness threatening to fall on top of her. The shadows of the commemorative military plates and the clay-horned toads mounted on her wall sank into the same darkness of the corners of the room. She didn't know where the soft light was coming from, but only that it must have been behind the figures surrounding her. They grew and shrank as she tried to form sounds and cries. Nothing. A self un-mouthed. Numb tongue.

Klea thought she was accustomed to her reoccurring sleep paralysis. She'd experienced it nearly every night since she could remember. She thought the dream intruders in her room were familiar by now. Familiar like the presence of bodies hustling around bus stations and grocery stores. There was always a space made in her half-sleep for some form to come to being. After breaking from her paralysis, she would remember it as if she were on the slab, an autopsy, and the intruder: a cataloguer of flesh and organ and the data offerings of bone.

Tonight's occurrence was different. The figures morphed and duplicated into a murky halo around her, instead of their usual dark errand of stillness and observance. She could not make out the faces or clothes, but they seemed to her to be shades of all the same family members from earlier that day. And instead of the tidal noise of storytellers, the figures were silent—voices held. A veil of quiet holding back a planet of sound—for now.

Klea could only whimper at them. No answering limbs or circuitry to help her jump from her bed and put the family figures back in a line. Back in a brightly lit room—that conference room in a hotel in Shiprock. A place for all the Tohonnie family members to gather. Four days she had been there. Video recorders. Laptops. Papers and pens. Anything to help document. Not for any agency or foundation, but for herself. She wanted to pull her people and their stories and connections, like streamers into one giant well-planned party. Many times she'd sped through Navajoland listening to her mother's stories. Her mom never took a break from talking at her. "Back there is your auntie Bess's first hogan with Rodge Cowboy," and "Your grandfather walked me through this field, corn and watermelon before the easement," and "Cousin Rita lived here but not for long, not long, I think." Those stories crowding Klea for hours—never hearing one specific family member's life story and no resting places between time, people, or events. She had stepped on the gas harder hoping to speed through the area. Speed to a destination with only one story: she at her uncle's with her mom. The new puppy litter, sandy and talkative. The cousin's baby boy quiet with a wide reach and strong hands for pulling hair.

No more winding and racing through her mom's stories. No more asking again to which of her grandfather's sixteen brothers a cousin belonged. No more sensing of rifts and bit lips and mental walkouts when other members of the family were mentioned or spotted near town as if they had stepped out of an ether of shame or past slights or lost journeys.

Her mother's explanations were a barbed wire warping and tightening along the washboard, red-dirt roads between Flagstaff and Shiprock.

But this family conference! This gathering! This "Stop by for a picture!" The great documentation! She would write down the names and dates of the sprawled and rising family. Would set up the laptop for those ready to record their own lines and connections. Would help the elderlies to softer chairs, warm cups of coffee, and would be patient— take in the sounds and smells of bodies busy with living, before she would point to pictures and ask who was who, and the wheres, and the whens.

To Klea this thing was an escape from trying to soak up all the stories. She could remember some moments here and there, but she could never remember the names, the areas, the faces. It was as if she was never built for stories that weren't on a screen, played out in front of her. As if the only stories she wrote were some one hundred-ish characters long or heavy with texting shorthand. Bits. Her notions of family scared her. Relatives would morph into giant immortals, too full of a presence to relate to—like the ones surrounding her bed, as she didn't yet sleep, but could not move or scream or seem to breathe. Her nightly ritual of horror: sleep paralysis. She entered a sleeping world as a waking being.

Today had been the last of the four days. She'd lost sight of the project and stumbled throughout the room. Talked out, she checked recording devices and took pictures. At first she'd captured as many relatives in a shot as possible, then walked over and wrote down everyone's name. Some she recognized from visits prior. Others from Facebook. One or two seemed like faces that were always around her in one way or another. A trace of family, a possibility space culled together from what must have been memory and resemblance.

In the corner of the conference room was a type of prison. It was her idea and no one—not her mother, not her closest aunt or most outspoken cousin—suggested she not do it. She was resentful when she looked at the corner—with its long blue sheet hanging from the wall, and to the side of it, a slouching table with her newly purchased clipboard. She wanted everyone's pictures. One at a time. Facing forward. Name on the clipboard, all the names: given, assumed, teased, and changed. Corralling the data, the dates and places of birth, when available.

No one went to the corner. No one asked about it. All Klea knew was that it was, somehow, a place of shadow. Why had no one said anything? Why do they let her do these criminal things that to her seemed to put the world into clearer spaces with borders and definitions? Facts. She just wanted to click on each relative's picture and understand immediately their place and therefore her place in this world. Her grandfather had sixteen brothers. Her grandmother sixteen sisters. This family, a jumble of yarn, didn't have to exhaust her the way it did. If only she could document—

When Klea could not sneak outside or to the bathroom, she drummed a line in her head: "At least we have plenty recorded. Plenty recorded. Plenty recorded." The drumming came at the height of her anxiety—when her hands felt like shaking and when she began to notice too many things, like the smell of horses and peppermint or the gang tattoos she could only assume made sense in another type of family—one pulled together through blood ritual and world-dreams. When she began vibrating into a panic, she was drawn to the crushed red velvet of her great-great auntie's blouse. Wanted to hold it between her fingers and think of bimá sání and how easy it was to just sit near her silently. Never needing to know anything, but what it felt like to take up a space next to Grandma and to smell of coffee and flour. To rush to the barrel of water outside the hogan and fill a tin mug with cool water. Shoo away the kitten at her foot.

Great-Great Auntie isn't correct. The terminology, that is. *What am I to her?* Klea thought and tugged her jeans back up from falling off her hips.

Auntie Evie squeezed her hand and leaned in close. When Evie spoke, Klea's vowels took a new shape. Some ended more abruptly. She paused more when speaking. Threaded words and dragging sounds disappeared and instead, she found her language slowed to plateauing formations. She spoke with the shape of the mesas surrounding her grandmother's home, flat and even, then a slow rising to a new type of flat and even—one closer to the sky. Evie's lips and chin clenched briefly as she motioned to the elderly woman. Her voice dropped. She said the woman told another cousin yesterday that Uncle Tyrone Jr. was not really one of the brothers. Evie's voice trailed off and she mumbled and giggled while still squeezing Klea's hand.

The last group of people to leave took the rest of the food with them. Klea and her mother helped carry the sandwich meats and breads, the muffins, soda, and uncut watermelon to their car and piled it all in next to a bag of dog food and some school supplies. Just moments before when Klea could no longer remember the name of anyone she met that day and was wishing for the firm squeeze of her aunt Evie's hand, Klea's mom had rushed up to her still talking to herself. Mid-story. Something about a playfriend her mother remembered, if only slightly. A girl she would call "big sister" and a corral with a billy goat that wouldn't stop yelling and bucking. They called the goat Shideezhí after the girl's younger sister whom they would hide from until she was so mad she'd yell and throw rocks at them as soon as she found them.

She met the new "big sister" and her daughters and a young boy that was in the care of one of the daughters though it was unclear to Klea why or how. As her mom chattered away at the woman and her daughters, Klea smiled politely and wrote down the names of each person in the group, but the letters were caught up in one another and she knew she wouldn't be able to read her own handwriting later. When the young boy began tugging at one of the daughters and pleading to her that it was time to go, Klea mentally began doing the same to her own mother. The group was nice, but for Klea, she had long since hid inside her a self that welcomed new friends and new family. Instead, she simply wanted some factual reality. Who was who. Where was where. When was when. The young boy's hand was sticky from a gumball and Klea opted to kiss the little fellow on the check instead of shake his hand. A brief moment with her lips close to his face, his cheeks plump and fresh, his skin smelling a little sweat-stained, but also wind-worn: like he'd stuck his head out the window during the drive for whatever reason the young seek a wind that drowns out all else but the blood of the working body. Klea's instinct was to scoop up the child and run off with him for more trading post fire gumballs and to nap in the shade. The sound of bimá sání spitting sunflower seed shells pulled fresh from the past to the now.

As Klea and her mom gathered up the disposable cameras, they counted two missing, but found two neon pink hair clips. They also found a scarf—not the soft and lustrous kind bought from a trendy corner of the internet, but the sheer and itchy gauze ones that her grandmother tucked between her mattress and the wall of the hogan— the ones she had thrown around her head and tied under the chin in a whip of a moment.

When it came time to take down the corner photo area, Klea stumbled over there alone; she swore and sweated and tugged at the sheet when it caught here and there on the generic framed prints of mesas and sand dunes that adorned the walls of the hotel reception hall. She was clumsy as she tried to silence the still-too-loud whisper of cotton sheet against the hardwood floor. She folded the paper from the clipboard and tucked it into her back pocket, not wanting to throw it away, fearful someone might spot it in the trash.

Klea's mom found the event to be a success. She gushed as she listed the people and interrupted herself with branches of stories or notes of interest. An uncle was unable to come, but he sent a list of people he remembered to be his cousins when he was younger, before his mother died and his stepmother died and the woman that lived with his father for several years unmarried died. The list was buried in the backseat next to notebooks and folders and her mom's last-minute road trip kit of bandages and safety pins and homemade round neck pillows for all the grandmothers. They buckled up slowly, arms exhausted and distracted by the sudden end of sound and movement and sugared pastries.

"Can you believe it?" her mom repeated. "I just can't believe it."

Klea didn't stop nodding, cracked the window and took in the dry road air, held it in her chest until it burned. She used her turning signal longer than she needed to and she snapped at her mother each time she was told where to turn or how fast to go when Klea already knew the way and could read the signs.

Back at her mother's house, Klea was grateful (and only somewhat ashamed by it) when her mother finally mentioned having a headache from the excitement and Klea set a small cup of Diet Coke and some Ibuprofen next to her mother's bed. She turned the TV on low and closed the drapes. "I'm glad we didn't have the family here," her mother said. "I told you there wasn't enough room here. And now we can rest." As Klea closed the bedroom door behind her, she could hear her mother's cell phone whistle and woo and her mom's winged voice start once again, mid-story, mid-life, mid-whisk.

I'm horrible. Klea knew and repeated this as she changed into her PJs, as she flew through TV stations, recognizing almost every show by just one character or the music or the setting. And she certainly knew she was still a horrible person later that night when she lay paralyzed in bed with the morphing beings around her. They didn't move closer to her on their own, but the room began to shrink and soon they seemed almost on top of her. She couldn't stop the space around her from retreating. Instead she whimpered and found her throat full of wool.

Klea jerked awake and scared off the small long-haired chihuahua that was nestled up against her thigh. She could hear the click click of the creature's claws as he skidded out of the guest room and around a corner and nudged at the bedroom door where her mother was (hopefully) asleep. She turned on the bedroom light, urging the disappointed and waiting figures from the room.

She could use a site like ancestry.com or perhaps build her own family chart through any one of her design programs. She could write it all out on a large piece of paper. But the idea of compressing her family history into data or lines on a page felt cheap and easy. Klea did not want to feel cheap nor did she want to be the kind that takes the easy road. She wanted to be the sort of person to go to a four-day gathering with her own blood and not so much flit about like her mother, but perhaps sidle up to people and smile and make them feel at ease. Her older brother could always do such things, but could never get time off of work, and actually if he had been there, Klea would have felt even more incompetent than she already did.

No, she wanted something organic. Some way of remembering that her mother seemed to have. Some way of grasping these histories and planting them inside her to let them grow and show their own signs of genus and pollination. Klea wanted to be an earth thing, something of soil and water. Of coded and bursting cells. And of light-made, force-made trembling, growing branches.

"Like a fucking family tree," she said aloud.

Klea slumped and cried. She felt like she was five and crying over nothing in particular, like she wanted to drop the thing she was crying over and let it crack against the floor when it fell . . . only to cry harder.

The kind of tears only another child would have: a fresh, heavy wetness to them that comes from nearing an absence in one's life, a space not yet ready to be filled with alcohol or work or gossip or feel-good and horror movies or even an addiction to serving others. Perhaps that adopted or foster-care boy would recognize such crying as his own. His black hair and skin the color of pinon shells reflected in those around him, but tugging at the adult nearest. His forced inclusion into the room of voices murmuring and sometimes a singer. Sometimes a singer out of nowhere like her grandmother's blind and half-paralyzed sister would sing. The middle of a conversation. The middle of a car-ride. A tremble song. The young boy and Klea never knowing what is going to happen next—do they shut up and listen? Do they sing along? Should her younger sister stop giggling? And instead looking out the car window, heads pressed to the cold glass, watching the long song of sand and blushing pink rock, the occasional curious horse looking back at them. And the way Klea would yank at the old Wagoneer's window handle and stick her head out as they neared her grandmother's home. Yell at the dogs to stay clear from the tires and hop out before the car came to a complete stop. She and that now-and-always family boy sharing a planet, sharing a sun.

In the dining room of her mom's house, Klea scribbled the young boy's name and the names of the people he was with on a notecard and tacked it to the wall. This, her mother's "I call her big sister" family. She included Shideezhí the goat on the corner of the card. She began shuffling the rest of the note cards until another name came to her. Klea wrote it down and tacked it to the wall. As the names started piling up and more details from the last four days popped into her head here and there, she wrote everything on cards and tacked them close to a name or in another section of unknowns. Someone had new shoes the color of asphalt and pink neon. Another had dimples that threatened to swallow the rest of the young girl's face. On a note card, the types of smiles: smirks, full and lipped; the smells: hay, coffee, the distinct smell of freshly printed paper, tobacco, rose perfume, flour, and cedar. The overheard words and phrases, the woman that always nodded, the man that was always leaning, the other man that would take her hand, but instead of shaking it, would hold it with both of his as if to hold her rather than greet her. All the partial-handshakes, the soft hellos. The names, so many boarding school names: Luther, Jermaine, Dorothea, Erwin, Neil, Laverne. And then Many-Goats, Nez, Yazzie, Tapaha, Singer.

Her purple marker ran out of thick ink-soaked lines and Klea rushed to find a red one. A black permanent one. And string. Yes, string. Before she could forget, Klea fastened the end of the string from one name to another. Sometimes pulling the string taut, sometimes too much and cursing while she re-fastened the string to the first card. Sometimes the string had to arc over other strings or droop down to the floor when she couldn't recall much more about the person. She used white string and blue. Sometimes yellow and black. As she moved around the room, she'd glimpse a pattern and lose it again. She'd feel a momentum building and lose it to a long battle of weaving strings and cue cards and repositioning. No no no, Vince is related to the Chinle area people though he came from Red Lake. No no, this sister is really the mother someone said. But too young, so too young to be a mother then. She is only mother, here on this wall and along the hushed conversation of the four-day gathering. As if the side talk and the hints and questions had tumbled from the great gathering into these threads of Klea's made graceful, but solid. Soft, but structural.

In this dream of making—this surge after her paralysis—the sun did not rise, and when Klea felt done enough to sit back into the archway to the dining room, she could not help but imagine herself a clever, spinning thing. An ancient thread-generating incarnation. As if she did have eight legs to smooth these lines throughout the room.

As if she was blessed with many eyes, small and large, light-absorbing rows of them to take in the work of the room. With more practice, with more time, with more blessing ways, she could learn to weave this thing into funnels, orbs or sheets. Pull the loose bits tighter and adjust the corners.

A family tree, she thought. How absurd. How unnatural. As if a branch of her bloodline could ever end. As if a tree was still a tree without sensing a forest. As if there could never be family in the treeless parts of the desert. Rather, this web. Stronger than steel, but slight and delicate. A ballooning thing. A thing made and remade and recovered and made new throughout generations. Split generations, lost ones, folded ones, brightening ones, all. And the only thing prey to this pulsing system was that version of Klea who built a photo ID area—an internment, that cold preservation of letters and numbers and attempts to capture the surface of a person. That fly. The resurrected census, a nothing process compared to this heavy dance of thread.

A ROBOT STORY

"I'll wait," Celee said and pulled out her copy of *Middlesex* to prove it. The woman at the lobby desk shook her head and sad-smiled at Celee and whispered back into her headset. Only a dozen other people had been there this morning and each of them arrived and left through the lobby happy and hopeful. Pamphlets or binders in their arms, they walked through the arched and windowed ceiling and across the silver and green tiles. One of the only buildings left boasting original plantlife, the lobby smelled a little old-world to Celee. And she liked it that way.

She pulled out yesterday's videostream and rewatched the thing in her kitchen standing there. His blinks and breaths in her absence were simple luxuries in this model, meant to ease her into a comfortable acceptance around this pseudo-husband. The dishes done, the counters wiped, the grease splatter from the stove no longer threatening a grime to ignore for another day. An invitation to someone's wedding squarely on the fridge, magnet oh-so-centered and complimentary. *Where'd he fucking find that?*

Though they knew him well—a little too well even, she sent in the photos and paperwork of her late husband along with a list of all the ridges, fats, and moles of him. The stretchmarks her new companion arrived with looked realistic, as did some of the skin tags. But the moles were always almost nearly alike one another in texture, and she remembered there was a particularly troubling green one she would often stare at while inspecting his hairline and ear. "Ow," he'd say and push her hands away and when they wouldn't stop, he'd pull them into his own and hold them sweetly, but firmly. She'd wrestle a bit, nip his ear with her tongue or lips, and roll back over away from him and they'd talk of the days behind and ahead and sometimes one would say something so funny, they'd giggle themselves back awake, and sometimes one would wonder if the other thought of having sex, but too tired-content-clumsy-close to sleep to suggest it, and then the other would curse the late hour with morning work approaching. Twenty-six years of such and it never changed, or got old, or felt as empty as it did with this new model. Though he was better at baking and letting her fingers trace the softest parts along the underside of his arm without squirming.

In the paperwork, she had described her late husband's strengths, flaws, common phrases, behavioral ticks, and even the dreams she remembered him telling her. She'd added sections on their rituals and even offered to come in and act it all out for the engineers. She'd turned in his phone, laptop, notebooks, letters, and all the childhood schoolwork his mother had cared to keep (though there wasn't much). Every photo, every video, every voicemail she could harvest from various databanks and friend's voicemails. Her husband's work colleague wasn't as forthright handing them over, and as Celee pleaded she began to feel that Jill had something to hide. No matter. He had been a friendly, flirty guy and never really noticed when other women were hitting or crushing on him. Even in his later years as his gut expanded and those worrisome ingrown hairs and red-sore pimples continued to romp about on his back and shoulders.

His gut was as wide as her husband's had been. It pulled at his shirts the same way, it indented the bed in the same way, and when she held him, it kept her fingertips from barely touching behind his back. But there was something about the squish of it that was wrong. And this along with the lack of color/texture variation of the moles, and the pimples and skin flaws that it magically applied, removed, and applied again were only reminders of how not-her-husband the thing was.

Satisfaction Guaranteed. Small writing. Little asterisks and daggers after certain words. Oh, she knew the lawyers would try to remind her that he wasn't ever going to be a real replacement and oh, they'd point to how much they were able to do for her the previous times she'd taken the thing back, but she wouldn't stand for it. And as her personal customer service guide and another man (small, but lean) walked toward her, she could tell they knew too.

Celee didn't actually have her own personal customer service person, not really. It was just that Lexi remembered her after the first two calls and when Celee requested her, she always happened to be available. Lexi had a way of putting her hand on Celee's and leaning in and speaking as if no one else could hear them and this was something that Celee knew as a way of "handling" her, but was thankful for this equation of intimacy nonetheless. The other man with her, though, did not seem like a handler, but a teller and a doer and perhaps he'd be the one to go over the fine print and close the door.

"Celee, this is James Stells. He's a great friend of mine here and he'd like to sit in on our conversation today. Is that okay?"

Celee agreed but steered close to Lexi as they made their way through the enormous lobby and maze of halls and offices to a room that she had never been in. It was snug up to one of the lobby's vaulted ceiling corners and the window in the room went from top to the floor. She could stand at that window and peer back down in the waiting area, the ceiling of the lobby now level with the floor of the room, and some feet of steel surrounding the lobby's glass ceiling before it ascended into a new arch. The slate-green tiles of the lobby formed an infinity sign with the company's logo in the center among the silver ones. The perfect floor for guests to see the expanse of the atrium and lobby without thinking of its terrifying distance through a glass-encased nothingness to a hard-patterned floor rushing from below.

Someone brought in her favorite tea (honey chamomile) and some fruits and crackers. Lexi gestured for Celee to sit down and since there was no cold metal table like in the rooms she was familiar with at the place, Celee chose the chair nearest the window and tried to settle in. Her two companions pulled their chairs closer and the food and tea on the coffee table between them meant Celee was constantly reaching forward and breaking the easy comfort of the chair. Always a little off balance. The other two avoided the teas, water, and snacks all together.

"Aside from the torso imperfections—"

"Inconsistencies," Lexi corrected Dr. Stells.

"Yes, sorry. Aside from that, Celee, I wonder if you would mind telling me a little bit about your interaction with Gorge."

"Gorge was my husband. This isn't him. It's pseudo-Gorge."

"That's not a name. Do you call him that every time?"

"Most times. Sometimes Sue. Sometimes George. When it's late and I'm tired."

"Let's stick with George."

"Or toaster."

"So, when you and George are together—do you use the adaptable mode installation?"

"Lexi, its stomach is off. It feels like sand in there. Wet sand. Do you fill these things with wet sand?"

"It's a silicone-based—"

"It's not an 'it,' Celee. It's Gor—George."

"Who the hell is this guy, Lexi?"

The AC in the room kicked on again and unlike the old buildings, the soft hum of it lasted only a second before it fell soundless and undetected. A manufactured silence to be exact, a wavelength used in the newest buildings that masked the sound of things turning on and off and clunking and manifesting themselves daily. After a night of cocktails or various wines, Celee would turn on the silence mode of the model and snuggle up to the machine and wonder if there was such a thing as manufactured time as well.

"Celee, I provide counseling for our clients as well as employees and really anyone interested in synthetic living partners. It can be an adjustment for so many of us. We know we aren't replacing any-one—they can't be replaced. But we do hope to alleviate some of the pain and—"

"Inconvenience."

"—obstacles. The obstacles of having lost someone."

Celee pulled her bag closer to her and slid to the end of her chair. "I've been to grief counseling. I've friends to talk to. This isn't about me or my grief or my experience as a widow. It's about my rights, as a customer. Satisfaction guaranteed."

"Yes, but—"

"His stomach feels like wet sand."

"Celee, we just—"

"And his zits are all a little weird. A little off."

"We are looking into it."

"And his breathing, his Sleep Apnea Mode is so goddamn predict-able! Have you ever had a partner with sleep apnea? It's impossible to sleep because at any minute the snores will kick up a notch or his caught breath will last forever. It's unpredictable even when it feels patterned. I sleep fine with this hunk of . . . silicone."

Celee smiled and squinted at Lexi and only felt the smallest bit of remorse when Lexi swallowed something sad and hurt.

Dr. Stells picked at the snack tray and offered Lexi a strawberry. They exchanged looks, and nods. The doctor's body tensed and relaxed and he moved a hand towards Celee. "I think Lexi can take it from here, Celee."

As he walked out, Lexi stood up and walked over to the window down at the vast lobby below.

"Celee, as we've discussed before, we are happy to take George—him off your hands. Our policy is to refund up to three months after purchase price—"

"Never paid for him."

"Yes, these circumstances are . . . were different, but nonetheless, we can't necessarily give you the money you would have paid since you signed the agreement and as we've made so many custom changes to the model."

"The contract I signed—"

"Damn it." Celee hadn't seen Lexi redden before, in splotches, along her neck and cheek before a tight paleness took over again. "Contracts. We're beyond that now. Compensation can't—could never translate directly. We were just trying . . . perhaps we were too eager in finding a substitute for your husband as part compensation. We all cared for you both. He was a wonderful man and we all miss him too, you know. So maybe we . . . well, we overshot it here, Celee. We just all tried too hard."

"And?"

"Well, there are other models out there—nothing that's on the floor now. We could talk about an earlier companion model, one whose functions are dictated by room assignment or travel assignment."

"Like a waiter?"

"Or chef. Or maid. Or driver. Or outing companion. Or . . . bedroom companion."

"Pass."

"Or yes. This next part might be tricky, but we do have prototype models, Celee. And you are so very experienced at turning in notes and suggestions and advice with our Reconsideration Department. Perhaps rather than provide any one model for its existing duration, we instead rotate new prototype companions? Now, some are just ideas we are tossing about."

Celee knew not to flinch. If Lexi mentioned kids, she knew not to flinch or redden or tighten or hold her breath. Gorge wouldn't. He wouldn't.

"—new invented family members—long-lost dads and siblings no one knew they had, disabled or ill companions that require a little care, but not too much. These are just ideas we've had that may or may not provide useful in certain circumstances. They aren't . . . they aren't ready for the public. You should know that now. They are just ideas. The children especially." Lexi closed some distance in her words and tried to swarm Celee. "We can't replace a child for a child, we won't." Lexi looked up the center of the building to the administration floors above, watched the long fall again to the glass arch below. "Not yet, but we hope they will surrogate, well, other losses. The children, though, they can be . . . tricky."

"Are these the sort of circumstances my husband was involved in?"

"I really can't be—"

"Please." Celee moved closer to Lexi, almost ready to grab at her arm or face or shoulders before pulling herself back into her own space and body. "Lexi, I don't care what he was doing here, but he was here and I didn't know and that means something to me."

At once the lobby, the arched glass ceiling, and the new view of the rooms above seemed less building than fortress. Command Center. Celee shook off the feeling of being watched though she was certain she was recorded, scanned, and stored somewhere by now in their files. She shook off the feeling that there are monsters and things she might not want to know about and her late Gorge knew her well enough to keep such things tucked away from her. In her early years of working alongside Gorge, Celee could always detect a dark secret among the codes and wiring and programs they created. Something too real in it, a place where they might lose themselves.

"Yes, your husband had an eye for certain improvements and his expertise in coding and platforms came in handy. Maybe nothing like this necessarily. But close to it."

"Whores? Military? Sacrificial fucking virgins?"

"Celee, you've such an imagination. I'm talking about very small adjustments. Almost uncanny. He understood something about subtlety, I think. About the small things that shape a person or event. Things undetected."

"Did he understand that when he dove out the window?" The widow had moved towards the window herself and was looking up several flights to where she imagined her husband must have been to clear the steel surrounding the lobby. Her middle finger along her bottom lip, a slight movement—one Gorge always performed when mimicking a worried Celee.

Lexi continued looking at the lobby before she swallowed hard and turned back to the woman. "You're probably exhausted. Why don't we get you home, power down a bit, and we'll send someone around in the morning for the model."

"He's in the trunk."

As the likeness of Gorge was wheeled through the lobby, the staff and employees stood still until they fretted with the hem of something or squeezed tighter around their binders or licked their lips one time too many. The side entrance seemed a more appropriate location for such transportation, but a new shipment of synthetics was lined among the halls and loading dock as they were moved into the crisp and kept air of the shipping vans. The lean bodies and fine hair and penetrating gazes of this newer model would have made the older that much more real for all watching. His paunch, his wrinkles, his splotchy skin and wisps of hair. Delia in Accounting sought to reach for him as he was wheeled through the hallway next to the employee breakrooms on Floor Eleven. The service elevator full still, the model made his way to the employee elevator and Bruce, the man with the dolly, began to wonder why they didn't just turn the damn thing on and make him walk up there himself before he heard an "Oh" from behind him. Jonny was both startled and stunned upon seeing Gorge again. Longing to hear the laugh and jaunts of the man again. No one knew precisely what Gorge did for the company, but his presence couldn't have gone unnoticed. His bi-monthly visits became weekly visits last fall, and unlike the administrators on the top floors, Gorge smiled at everyone and spoke to whomever was closest to him. The last sort of man you'd expect to take a thirty-floor dive to the cold concrete floor below. The new tile did its best to erase the blood spill everyone had ample view of for too many hours.

And though Celee had agreed to give up the synthetic without a second thought, she still wanted a chance to say goodbye to the damn thing. And though Dr. Stells would have rather had her meet the thing on the floor she had been held on, reserved for customers and guests, Lexi had already ordered Bruce to take it to Floor Twenty-Nine where the model reconstruction team would have a chance to log it in—no models enter the building without logging in. They sped through the process to get them to the next floor and into a small room that was once called a conference room, but without enough space for a long table or adequate AV equipment, it simply became a kind of waiting room that everyone hated or tried to use as a break room.

It was only as Celee was entering the room did she realize it might have been the exact same one Gorge had burst out of that winter morning. She thought she saw Lexi tighten up only briefly, in a blink barely caught with her eye. Lexi inhaled and steadied her breath, wishing for a shield against any detection. "The rest of the floor is so noisy and anything above this will need more clearance."

"Did Gorge have that type of clearance?"

"No, he was a consultant. As I've said."

"For what?"

Gorge stood in the middle of the room. Unresponsive. Cold. Only eerie to those outside the urban areas that had not managed to see this tech launch some years ago.

"He's so much like him," Lexi said.

"Is he?"

"Well, yes. I mean. The things you remember aren't what we remember, Celee. But before he'd smile or laugh or show some warmness to him, there was this cold quietness in him. I'd catch him now and then ... in the hall ... just thinking, I guess. Just seeming so alone. He felt very alone. And often. But the logs you provided and the details you gave, it seemed you were both very much in love and had . . . a good partnership."

"Yes, but there were things. There are always things. This place. His coworker Jill, maybe. I dunno. He said he was happy, but I always suspected. Something lost long ago in him." Celee shook the thought out of her head, scratched her nose that wasn't itching. A fuzz in her that almost had an outline of the past before it disappeared. A child's outline.

"Was he always like that? Can you remember, Celee?"

"No, no. He was a very stable and grounded person for many years before. I'm not sure what happened to him."

"Hmm. Well, let's turn him on and you can say your goodbyes."

"He is on."

"He's just standing there."

"Yes."

"Initiate welcome, Gorge."

He continued standing. And staring.

"Initiate conversation, Gorge."

There was nothing. Nothing but a silence beyond the silent mode.

"He's had some adjustments, I think."

"No, it is a fine job of programming, I think. The adaptability mode, I think. He's adapted a new silence, maybe we both have."

"Initiate adaptability termination."

Nothing.

"Adaptability program report."

Gorge's mouth moved. "Adaptability began four months, six days, and three hours ago. No down times. Boosts weekly."

"Adaptability boosts? Who could—"

"You wouldn't tell me anything," Celee said. A small plea stuck in her throat. "I just needed to see it again. To know, really know."

The machine took its first steps toward the glass window.

"It's just that it seemed to come out of nowhere and there was no way to tell what he was thinking or why he was thinking it."

Gorge reached for Celee and pulled her close. The scent of his hair and sweat only slightly off from her real Gorge. The new sag to her skin almost too perfect.

"I just wanted to know," she said and held on.

The pound against the glass wasn't like that of Gorge. Gorge couldn't penetrate it quickly and it took some chairs and a small end table to break the glass as others pulled and pounded at the secured door. Gorge's letter to Jill on the table and all his papers signed and squared away to her. His home office a fit of papers and the heat of his computers and the sadness that comes when a future ends. A small childthing in the corner. Its laughter and pouts and playfulness torn out of it. That violence of sound removed from the empty empty of the house.

But this machine hit into the glass in a stride and a half, the room too small to contain this speed and strength of math and exponential possibility. And the crash of the glass sent a rain of shards down past the office windows. Widowers and the lonely and their supportive tech teams rushed to this new sound—this breaking of their secure worlds. As Gorge's body plunged down, many thought they already knew this, already lived this, only this time the small body of a woman and the way her dress flapped above him seemed entirely separate from their memory despite the comfort in seeing them cradling one another.

THE LAST SUPPER

You'd be amazed how many last meals consisted of fried, greasy, or fatty foods. Robert Alton Harris, who kidnapped and killed two young boys, one shot point blank in the face, requested a last meal of a twenty one-piece bucket of Kentucky Fried Chicken, two large Domino's pizzas, a six-pack of Pepsi, and a pack of Camel cigarettes. With brain matter still on the barrel of the gun hours after the killing, he boasted to a girlfriend about shooting the boys while chowing down on a hamburger. Later, he described with much pleasure the last pleas from one of the boys to an arresting officer, who happened to be the boy's father. Harris also asked for a bag of jellybeans and ice cream with his final meal. Looking through a long online list of hamburgers, fried chicken, pizza, subs, pies, candy bars, and a dozen deep-fried shrimp (the shrimp requested by John Wayne Gacy), two last request meals stand out: the sugar-free pecan pie and sugar-free walnut ice cream ordered by convicted murderer Clarence Ray Allen along with his meal and the unaccompanied two pints of mint chocolate chip ice cream requested by the withdrawn, suicide-seeking, self-imposed vengeance-dealing Timothy McVeigh. Mint chocolate chip—which happens to be my favorite ice cream as well.

June and I aren't convicted murderers. We cater to a palate that has been flushed with years of carefully planned breakfasts, brunches, lunches, linners, dinners, desserts, and midnight snacks. We enjoyed all the things outside a 6x8 prison cell, but couldn't help checking in on the experts to devise our fabulous Last Supper menu. It's a game we play. It's the end of the world and you feel fine ... what will you eat for dinner? It's the end of the world and you feel fine ... which album will you play on repeat? You'd think our last meal would be just as filling as the time we discovered that little family-owned Hawaiian BBQ shack downtown or any Crabfest buffet—June is tenacious when it comes to crab. Instead, the meal—an overly spicy and somewhat underwhelming array of Thai-sprung veggies and grilled chicken—just sits in us ... at least in me, sinking. And pulling any feelings of fullness or satiation into a heavy, churned pit.

"Maybe we should have just made something we know we liked," she offers and twirls her hand in the Scrabble tile bag longer than usual. "You know, instead of being fancy." June always takes an extra few seconds to pull her tiles from the bag, as if in those moments the letters she needs will find their way to her. Sometimes they do. Mostly they don't. And I play words like *CUNT* and *BOOGER* to keep myself entertained.

I wait for her to place her tiles on the rack and move them about. Seeing. Spelling. Finding. Calculating. *It's the end of the world, what game do you play?* I also imagine some pre-planned romance tonight as well. Like it is the last time, she'll say. *It's the end of the world, where will you kiss me first?* Though, in all honesty, this morning's quickie had been it for me. June is too emotionally fragile by the end of the day and I think she forces herself to be more than she is up to being. In the mornings, though, she's been up with nightmares or woken with the "what was that?" startles, and her lack of sleep does her a little justice, she's receptive and looks to me. She doesn't flinch and can relax when

I pull her close. At least, I think she relaxes—she seems to, the poor girl—poor *us* really. In the evenings though, she has been created over by the day. Flashbacks of a recent sexual assault catch her in tiny, unmonitored moments. Throughout the day she feels herself swell with confusion and fear, then reins herself into a small walnut of herself. Her insides, still earthly sweet and surprisingly tender to me. And that shell! Hard—an angry hard. But for me at least, there's always a suggestion of how I might crack into her, guided by that seam. Her thin lips pursed. *It's the end of the world, which nut do you think I am?*

I hold back from placing a seven-letter word that would allow an *X* to fall on a double-letter score. *EXAMINE.* I'm afraid she'll catch her breath once she reads it. Either from the score or the idea of someone's eyes and hands all over . . . well, all over anything. She stopped eating her chocolate croissant the other day when a fellow patron was consuming his with flakes tossed about his shirt and face. He, hunched over the pastry, eating it like it would be his last, which actually . . . it might have been. His own End of the World game. But I stopped eating as well. The croissant, undone by the haphazard bites that remind us all that a croissant is and always was only made up of layers of itself. Crisp, flakey layers with nothing inside to treasure or suck on. Just layers undone.

I play *MAIN* and hold onto that *X* thinking I can find a triple letter placement (hopefully, by an *I* and with an additional *I* on my rack to use for a sixty-plus point word whopper). But I know I probably won't use it. We are going to play this game and June will win. She won't pulverize me though, she'll know what I'm up to if she does.

I can't believe I called her a nut or worth breaking into. Sometimes that type of language is the only thing I can find in me—reinforced year after year from too many sources around us to count. There's only one nut I know of that might think of all women this way and I don't know anyone else who deserves being broken into more than that fuckface.

I can't look at June when I start to think of him or she'll see what I'm planning. And this game board becomes a sick place of strategy and movement and results, which asks me to get up and do something about this situation. *It's the end of the world, who would you hunt down?* I look outside, but the sky is holding a thick and moody grey and it is probably quite poetic to those drifting these hours. The sun breaks through the cloud cover at times and the sky says many things about its wayward charms. It has secrets, but it likes to remind us it is willing to share them. I wonder if he is looking to break into the sky as he did her. Fuckface, we call him. Because we can no longer say his name.

Fuckface is possibly drinking or raping a girl.

In all the days I think of him, he is usually drunk and raping a girl. 4:35 a.m. June is groaning in her sleep and he is drinking and raping a girl. 11:28 a.m. I am at work and wondering if June is moving throughout her day well enough and he is drinking and raping a girl. I try to get home quickly, worried I will find him there. Drinking and raping a girl. I check the newspaper often. Drunks. Raping.

June plays *VESTITURE* off the word vest. It's only for thirteen points, but it looks impressive. We've no rules on archaic terms. She says it's what they used to call clothing. I nod. I have no idea what most of the words I spell are. It's a word game for June and her literary expertise serves her well. But it's a numbers game for me, and with a trusty dictionary nearby, I usually win.

In my letters are throngs of violence. *HIT. TIE. VEX. VIE.* And that blank tile making it worse: *BITE. EVIL. HITS. THIEF.* Even *EXIT* or *SEX* seems vulnerable to us on this board falling next to words like *NO* or *STOP* or *HELD.* When June plays *LOWER*, I add an *F* to the top. When she plays *CUT*, I play *CUTIE.* She tells me to knock it the fuck off.

I play *EXIST* and she smirks and looks outside. "We probably should have just made your baked cheesy noodles. My favorite." With her sitting there taking all our games too seriously, probably unseeing some magnificent seven-letter word to drop on a triple score, and her dinner thick inside her, her body turning it round and round and finding no nourishment or pleasure, I wonder what Fuckface is eating. What he is drinking. And raping. And eating while he rapes and drinks.

His last supper: something meaty, red, and dripping. He tears into morsels of flesh with those freakishly sharp and long teeth—strands of meat pulled close to the gum from the ripping and his refusal to slow down. Flesh caught. It probably doesn't even bother him. Juice on his hands, blood-run and salty. He, sweaty and grunting. Licking his lips. Saliva. A guttural laugh and those eyes of his drowned in whiskey, moving slowly side to side. I can't help it. This is what he is to me. There's no curve to him. No roundness. No nestling places. Just his body, taut and small with too many points to him. His thin erect dick, his jutting tongue and terrible claw hands. Those teeth, which sank into her breasts and genitals, over and over. Animal. Beast. Monster. June sees him as such in all her day and night dreams, but it doesn't seem too far off. She, every day, is still his last supper.

And I see it happening. *It's the end of the world, who would you kill?*

Me: "I think I'm going to go grab some ice cream. Mint chocolate chip?"

She: "Like McVeigh?"

Chuckling.

She: "I can go with you."

Silence.

Me in front of her: Waving hand. Grabbing my coat. Keys. Phone. Wallet—because I will have to get the ice cream on the way back. Me in the garage: grabbing a bat. Grabbing a large chunk of something metal, heavy, and, in my shaking hands, dangerous. June has urged me to find a support group. Or to talk to my buddies. I told her talking to my type of friends would only form a hunting party. I see me calling them. "Just need an hour of your time." Or, "I'll be there in five. Be ready." Or, "It's time." Or something—anything—not like the real thing would be, the dry and weak from too many tears voice, "I . . . ugh . . . I think I'm going . . . um . . . can you . . ."

We meet at the tattoo shop. There's gotta be time for this. In the last moments at the end of the world, there must be extra hours ready to be swallowed up and away from the real time. Hours that make sense to those few involved and to others, are just normal time. June is home in normal time. And me, here—no one can notice this small band and its dirty errand. We've all just left our warm homes, loves, and adorable children and pets for a brief hello is all. It's possible. We are close like that. And the gloves, the streetwear, the surge of adrenaline and testosterone, only a blip undetected on the scan of individual pulses and chemistries across the globe. Not just ignored, but possibly grant-ed—this small, wrought and angry hour of ours. As if the roads were clear for us. The phone lines open for us. The movement of weapon to body magnetic for us. Breath escapes through the vents of the car and is not nearly as foul as Fuckface's drunk, hungry, rapey gasps so many nights past. It is the breath of messengers. We do what we must.

And we don't say much. Then we don't say anything. He's at his house or a bar we know he frequents or at work. He's in all the easiest places to reach, another gift to us. And he's drunk and raping a girl. Perhaps he's lit candles and picked some baroque composition that under the circumstances suddenly seems rusty and stained with semen and vomit. Or it's a den, dark and cold, gnawed bones and the stench of urine all about. More than likely, it's just a normal place. Fuckface seems normal, the normal drunk and raping type. And before I can swing my bat at his soft shaved head, I grab the flesh from whatever stylish but attractive IKEA plate he's eating off of and shove it in his mouth. Not down the throat, not yet. But past the teeth and threatening the extent of his jaws. I pull him down to the floor and look into those eyes that seem to only say "I drink and rape girls."

His body is wiry. Still muscled and tense, but . . . little. As if he escaped from June's daymares and shrank with each step towards his home. The great mass of violence of him becomes pleated inside him, ready to blow up, only with enough hot air to expand across days and weeks and miles across the city to our very home when she closes her eyes. I push him down hard. Now harder. Fuckface arches his back and writhes. He's difficult to keep on the ground, but I've pounds on him and back-up. I continue shoving food down his mouth. His tongue fails him despite its effort to push back, to maneuver the flesh in him, to use itself to cry for help. I feel his panic: why won't his tongue work for him? He claws at my arms. The red marks along my arms, so familiar. I think, given time, I'd bruise the way she did. Taking weeks to fade from the ungodly blood-welt to a stain of yellow on her skin. And then to a memory only seen in a flash when she catches sight of herself in the mirror. My arms take the force of his hands. My muscles a new resistance to him. My weight, a new body to negotiate. He can't disarm or rock my balance the way he has learned to other bodies. He can't use my bones and tendons against me. He reaches for my face, but I can pull my head upwards and away, I can tease him a little—pretend he's close to me, but I've got him under me and when he tries to gain some ground with his legs, pulling up his hips and bending his knees to get the soles of his feet on the ground—to find a foundation, to make some use of himself, to fight back and hold—I slowly, methodically, feeling and encouraging each ounce of myself— push myself onto his hips with my bended knee. I won't climb on top of him entirely. I won't put myself right above him to see directly in his eyes or to know what it is like to hold someone to the ground like that, to have all of them in my grasp. I will give him a small chance, a moment to think he can break free, to imagine what it must be like to squirm from under me and, if time would have allowed, enough doubt for him to wonder always if he could have saved himself, if he had tried . . . just a little harder.

My hunting party is divided. *Do it.* More meat down his throat and his eyes will roll. His limbs will soften and that blood that has pumped through him taking him from bar to bar and girl to girl will no longer work. Dead, made impotent. Or *Make it last.* Work him a little less and a little less. Until he's half-living. The shell of a person. Tired, beat, always thinking if he could only breathe enough, only open himself up, and not find the weight of something or someone else in him, if only—he could move on and live a happy life . . .

"For eighty-two points," June says.

She adds an *S* to the end of *EXIST* and uses the *N* from my word *BEGIN* to lay *STAR_ING* on a triple-word score. Her body open and her face, half-smirk half-smile. She lays the letters carefully on the board with the little click of an expert. And she's no longer tucked into herself or yawning or wavering in her strength, but she is still here, still smiling, still present with me. She looks happy. A survivor. And I think maybe she's got it right and she's going to be okay. The word *STARRING* a possibility on our board—the collisions in her and this new gravitational pull around us will ignite heats and energies and molecular bodies. She's going to ascend to become part of the celestial. She'll revolve, evolve. Explode. Implode. And it will all happen light years away from us. Or *STARTING*. A new path. Or—

"Starling?" I ask. I imagine June's birdself—strong, direct, gregarious. Goes anywhere and hears everything—no longer recluse or nesting. The sounds of car alarms and the contagious laughter of children or the hopeful bleating of kid goats doesn't startle her and she learns all their sounds. Subtle and hidden as well as loud and expanding notes that she finds, figures out, and speaks. She sings all the languages now.

"Starving," she says. "Starving!"

She lifts up the pad of paper she is using to keep track of our points and shows it to me. She's 150 points ahead. "You better get in the game, friend. Don't go soft on me now."

"Right. But," I say, "then I'm going to go get us some ice cream."

"It's just a game," she says.

"It's the end of the world and you feel fine and which ice cream do you want?"

"Hmmmm. Mint," she says. Her face alight. "Mint chocolate chip."

SEVEN YEARS OF CUPS

After my wife had the third baby in the same hospital room we've been in for seven years, the nurses pulled out the baby clothes we used for the first two kids. Not all of the items kept together well. The thin blue cloth of hospital gowns cinched and manipulated into onesies and dresses and those pants with the snaps all along the bottom were spread out on top of my father's comatose body. It's not unusual anymore for us to use that space as a surface. It all started when we covered him in Christmas lights and stuffed the presents underneath his adjustable bed. Sometimes the world under my father is just storage.

This third baby is now eighteen months old and 21.5 pounds and 30.1 inches. Her audiologist is around often. Almost daily, he pokes his head in and asks what's for lunch while pointing to one of our discarded lunch trays. Tacos. Grilled chicken. Veggie lasagna. Today I say, "Roast beef." My cheery wife offers, "Chicken makhani and a cup of pepper rasam," and his smile broadens. We know none of us have had anything other than hospital food, let alone Indian, for at least seven years now. Nurse Maris brushes by him and he straightens up at the brief touch of her, then walks his long body entirely into the room and stops pretend-itching his ear. He winks at my wife.

I think they fuck down in the morgue. I've almost caught them twice in the large handicap bathroom on the fourth floor, Tower B.

"How's he doing today, Maris?" he asks, now folding his arms and pretending not to see my wife shift what little weight she has to her right side as she uncrosses and crosses her legs.

"He's wonderful," Nurse Maris answers. She pushes the middle child's Legos off of Father. A council of blue towers fall. She kicks them under the bed. The middle child doesn't cry anymore when his work tumbles off my father. He doesn't ask if Grandpop moved either. Once: Was that him? The child's eyes the size of petri dishes. But no more of that. No more Uh-oh when he rips out the IV. He just sticks it back in.

We have a third kid. The big one. Seven years old, 56 pounds, 47.7 inches. I don't know if they are a girl or boy. They tuck the hospital gown here and there to make pants sometimes. Sometimes they drape it. At first, I worried Father would wake up and see the kid and demand to know which he or she was. I played around with many answers. It is what it is, Dad, which is something I said a lot year three of living here. New people coming in and out of the room to check on us and me always answering, "It is what it is," and taking a razor to Father's gruff. But "it" as days or a life is not the same as a person. They are what they are, Dad, I'd say.

Actually, I haven't seen the kid in a few months. But I know they are around. The nurses say they are very helpful around here. They like to help with the filing and running down doctors and administrators with forms to sign. The kid needs some experiences outside this room. There's only our home and Father's shell to keep us busy in here. I used to impose some order on the room. I made a kitchen by the sink and even brought in a contractor friend. He measured up the place and wrote a bid. Then muttered about building codes and red tape. He was just trying to help out, but by the time the staff caught up with us, I'd already dug a needle through to his bone. Still seething. They don't let those things sit around anymore. And I've stopped worrying about building onto this home.

Eventually we just piled in here and let it be what it was. The kids learning what they could in other towers and from other patients and various aides and technicians. The cafeteria always open even if the lights weren't on. They'd shown us how to get through the locks. Whatever we needed. *Whatever you need*, everyone said. *Whatever you need.* I thought we could maintain this life pretty well, but soon my wife was down at the gift shop every day and talking about the garden between Towers A and B. I could see her down there from Father's room. At first, she met our friends and neighbors there, then other visitors, and then her lovers. Too many to count now.

Though I haven't actually caught her yet with the audiologist. I assume she thinks the morgue is the only part of this place I haven't seen yet. She couldn't be more wrong. I go down there every day when she takes her shower. It's cold like you'd imagine. Steel things like you'd imagine. But also, it's just a room. I lie on the tables and pull a sheet over me. Wait and wait. Wonder what waiting is to those that can't wait anymore. Does my father wait?

You won't believe the amount of fucking that happens in that room. The positions alone are ridiculous. I think it must be that no one wants to look very long at any one thing in a morgue, so there's all sorts of adjusting and flipping and balancing and always the closing of eyes. But the mouths clenched. You'd think they'd be open the way mouths and things want to be open and merge or open to release when touched. But really everything is tightly drawn up. No one wants the stale air of that place in them. They all want to feel alive. Once while hiding in a small nook near the lockers, I saw a dozen people in there. All up inside one another. All tongues and hands and genitals. The smell of recently sterilized utensils still in the air.

I have yet to find my wife there, though I'm sure she's soon to arrive. Everyone has been there at one point or another. Even the other coma patients are wheeled in, usually around holidays and when there was that heat wave a few summers back. I've been measuring the space between the wheel marks on the floor of my father's room and the wall to see if someone has carted him anywhere while I slept. Yesterday, I put a few chalk lines on the wheels just to see if they moved at all.

I'm very watchful in year seven, which wasn't always the case.

I imagine many would say floating through the first months of our new home wasn't the best move on my part, and maybe it has led to my wife's adventures with the hospital staff. We came in either to have the first baby or to watch my father die. I can't remember which it was. I just remember one day there was a baby in her and my father was awake and the next, the baby was out and Father was what he is now. I wanted to name the child after my grandfather, but my wife said the baby will "make their name known" within a few hours of holding and cooing and kissing them. But the baby never did or I wasn't there when it happened or maybe we were all back in my father's room at the same time and my father moved not a bit and the baby's name fell to the floor to be swept up with the candy and sandwich wrappers that littered this room for the next seven years. The middle child came with a burst of excitement that ended in another room while I held my father's hand and explained to him that things were going to change, that we'd need more room, that we didn't have enough money to keep things as they were, that letting go—letting go—there needed to be some letting go like letting the poisoned blood out and into plates and vials. Dark, slow, and misguided, but the best option for what we knew in that moment. But Father never said a word and this was his worst sort of disapproval and the third baby came and suddenly it had been many years since we left this place.

All the while there were kids dying around my kids and volunteer teachers carving out ten minutes here and there to teach them a thing or two and there were always still holidays. An Easter egg hunt that led to my father's bed and underneath were his unopened gifts from all the years before and the children's hand-me-down clothes and the names of my children and every recycled paper cup I used because I was too embarrassed to let anyone know I urinated in my coffee travel mug when I couldn't leave my father's side after I thought I saw his spirit escape into a heating vent only to roll back out with each new winter as soon as the cold bite hit.

While buying another *coffee—plain-coffee* with a nod to Lula, this week's barista, I watched her try to force more discarded cups into one of those super-thin and cheap garbage bags that we have started to use as strainers in our makeshift kitchen. From just one day there seemed to be a hell-of-a-lot of cups. So many so that seven years' worth of them shoved under the bed of my father seems to be a possible un-truth that has floated around inside me for so very many days.

In fact, the recycled paper cup can't be squished down so far as to allow for seven years of cups (eight to ten a day) to go unnoticed. And it might be that my father's bed could soon be stirred by this growing pile, which would then throw off the measurements of the bed's position in the room, which would then lead to a false reading of whether or not my father's body was being used in the morgue orgy like all the other forever un-peopled. And it's not that I want to deny the rights of my father to experience the last thrusts and gyrations of what we call life; he was a man that would do whatever he wanted to do, of course. But what feels so wrong is that my wife could easily be in the mix and wouldn't my children and I one day notice that both Grandpop and wife were gone for long periods of time and returned to us a bit lighter in step or with some sort of new happiness that comes from not being just shell people and wouldn't that be something awful to face? That sort of betrayal of having a life even if it was shoved into less than an hour of cum and worming?

The walls of Tower B no longer look coated in beige ants, but I can see there is an expensive-for-us embossed wallpaper along it that has grown its way from the oncology and baby care units towards the un-lifed Tower B floor where everything is wheeled in to be forgotten. The wallpaper runs out before my father's floor. And what it looks like to me is that someone in this building, some administrator who doesn't have to live here, wants to make use of extra building expenditures and there's always that push to make each tower and the entire conclave of these buildings and structures, this municipality of blue arrows on the ground and pink baby footprints along the walls into a thing of itself—a whole thing of itself. A nation. A country. As if we all are here under one banner and with one goal, which should be to get better and get the fuck out, I guess.

This isn't the first time I've been told this place no longer wants to house us or my father. This isn't the first time the space of my father has been called many things other than a man. And it's not the first time I've demanded we continue sustaining in this room, with this weight, with these items, and with the uncanny reassurance of Nurse Maris and that sleazy audiologist robbing our kid of her own language and culture and the hospital gown clothing and the terrible half-smiles of the volunteer staff.

By the time I pass the no-longer-weeping partner still next to his husband's bed in room 1053A, I can hear my father's bed rustling behind the closed door. Something tremor-like or a silence just itched at by sound and I look about to see if anyone else notices it but there is only the sound of one of my children running through another hall and throwing paper planes and that no-longer-weeping partner breathing and the carnival voices of all the televisions interrupted by a toilet flushing here and there. There's no one in this hall but me and my hand on the hospital room door and the ruckus is louder and even a little rhythmic like he's trying to ready his body to sit up and I half expect to hear my father yell "Where the hell am I?" or "Keep it down" or maybe just those angry grunts he made watching his team lose over and over again by bigger margins every season.

But instead the room seems empty of anything at first, even his body is just part of this emptiness and this home is no longer a home but suddenly a regular old room of lost everything. Until the sound picks up again and there's a sigh and a moan and a sucking of skins and someone biting a lip and I reach for the sheet over my father, which someone has draped inexpertly over him. And there under his bed are Nurse Maris and my wife, a tangle of body, and even as the nurse thrusts her hands and self into my wife, she is still so thorough, so deliberate—made of careful hands that changed my father's bedpan and dutifully rolled him from one side to the other and always friendly despite being overworked. This very keeper of us all, determined and warm and all-knowing. And the audiologist peeks his head under the bed from the other side and smiles and says, "How's he doing today, Maris?"

My wife cums like there's no tomorrow, the nurse's hand never skipping its beats, and Nurse Maris says, "He's wonderful. Just wonderful."

EPILOGUE: HOW WE HOLD THE DEAD

S ly sly sly! In threes, always. She thinks, sly sly sly!
    At the video streaming out in front and within her. Here the movement of bodies on boards, on bikes, on air with parachutes yanking out behind them. Bike the coastal rode, road bike the dirt womp, bike the mountain crush. Run the asphalt and scaddle rock clifferies. "Sly sly sly," She says and knows She's got the words wrong again. Wrong, off, and slump-like. And her grasp on the length of sentences and phrases and what what that thing that goes high and low like a tail at the end whipping and wooing. "Aye aye aye," the words a thing un-doing. But here the video, the stream, the data bits and She can catch them and ride them too.

"Be what you want to be."

Body on the surf. Body on the slates on the snow. Body on the—on the—in the wind and ache and speed of it all. The wind and whhhh of it all.

"If you dream it, you can be it."

The video-voice like a hail but a man and he has the deepening and he has the oat oat oat of it all and he says to eat the you and be the you and dream the you and She remembers She was once a You and this video could be for her-You, but it plays out in front of another—in front of The Woman in her late year, in her early morning clothes, in her just-waking head.

She and The Woman bound together watching. One body.

"If you dream it—" The Woman says to a no one, no one thing. And a no one, a nothing is a She that is no longer her own body and no longer a name, but a vibration space. And in threes and losing her words and feels the body go woosh on the video because She has learned to spread herself into the stream from the computer. Spread herself from the stream of time and space that the bodied people are using.

She is the sound of things and the caught air of it and the waves emitting. And sly sky high! That video with its message of doing and She thinks She can be a doing thing too. If only—

The Woman sips at her emptying coffee and the video shrinks to a smallness in the corner of the screen and the words *to dream, to be, to do, to imagine, to live* now cramped and the cramped pictures of bodies doing and also something of the stars and something of a deep meadow and soft soft soft the glow of hope. All cramped, corner screen. She is messed that the video plays in the corner now and not on the bigness in front of The Woman. In front of The Woman are the busy screens of messages and peopled boxes and The Woman is checking off her reading and The Woman is reply all'ing and the screen shows New, Likes, and red red red exclamation marks. But The Woman is still half-woke, half-dreamt and She knows it. Like She knows under the room is another room and under that is another room, but under that is a heft of limestone and sea fossils spun out with arms and things spun in with shell. And then there is a warmth and a nothing and a pulse and an ache and She knows The Woman is just a small thing to this larger thing around them. And The Woman's sleep has been a blessing to them both as her wake is a sludge and cramped expanse of time.

She pulls the video big and back and to the front of them, collapses the other bits of data and The Woman is No no no! and Oh shit! and What! and Ugh ugh ugh! and The Woman tries to open the busy ways again, but She wants the bodies in motion and the dream, the dreamness of bodies in motion and the meadow and the words of being a You that is the you You want to be.

Stupid thing, The Woman says and musses the mouse around a dull pad. Ugh.

The Woman takes coffee sips again and up the bottom of the cup because there is a no thing left and The Woman pushes her chair back and a huff and her feet are a stomping back to the kitchen. She doesn't yet follow, but She leans close to the screen message again and Follow Your Heart in a white swirly lettering and the body is jumping and there is the earth behind and the earth is thankful to the body in motion and the body is thankful to the lettering and whip whip whip. She knows there is heart to follow too. Stirring to mountain, to ocean, to air.

In the kitchen, The Woman is snapping her appliances and pulling foods out and into the pans around her and mumbling and her damn computer and the acting up and The Woman is a closed system to She. And She has grown tired of The Woman. But her tether leads her only close steps from The Woman and The Woman never ever leaves. There is no leaving.

They two are a nothing of nature. The She orbiting The Woman, but The Woman not a sun. The Woman not a planet. Not the earth, not even a moon and She not even a satellite. She is a meteor storm of stored once-self stuck to The Woman and The Woman cares little of the stars and the bodies in motion and the heart following. The Woman cares for the thing in the front of her and that thing is the pan and that pan is hot and that bacon is a sizzle and She knows this and cares too. Because within the sizzle are beads of air and they pop pop pop and on the skin they sizzle too and She imagines the air a buzz in the pan and if She can expand herself back into the sizzle and She can speed up the heat and the air and the sizzle and what explosion does that bacon make on the arm of The Woman so that The Woman stumbles and falls backward and slumps down after hitting herself against the counter and the slip of the floor. Enough now, She threatens. Enough now, The Woman sobs.

The Woman is too much a sadness about the loss of She. There is a tether from another woken day, one that held them together because in the world of bodies in motion there is something of a network of selves and those selves seek to self themselves to others. And She somewhat remembers this closeness, once treasured, that is now a quicksand. She cares little for the tether and the name and the calling and culling and space that was once The Woman and She. Instead, there is the following of sound beating and whirred and dreams like air filling her and odes "you can be it" and She thinks She can too. Can get to a there-in-motion, a there-in-all if there is no tether. If she is not named a space in a narrow human-world.

The Woman curses, cradles her arm, grease stainburn up and out to the nothing space. And says the once-name of She. And The Woman begins to think herself called upon to see something and do something and self herself to a new thing and all the words of those around her that said there is Moving On and that The Woman must continue to live because the once-She would want that. Those words come to her and The Woman has what these selves call an epiphany and isn't the world here to wake her up and that video that sprung sprung sprung to the screen and The Woman was unable to continue her duties so decided to feed herself. And when attempting this, The Woman had— The Woman very had—The Woman simply had been thinking that maybe there was more to life than this, than the grief and the work and the work of the grief and feeding oneself in a lonely way as a lone person without another and couldn't The Woman also be the kind to follow moving on? And The Woman raises her hand to the counter behind her because The Woman knows there is a phone up there and pat pat pat the counter to get to the thing metal plastic and her sight is many and The Woman calls her friend and says along the lines of the weirdest thing just happened and I think once-name is trying to speak to me and do you believe in ghosts?

And She is working at that tether and thinking there is a gnawing that must happen to break it apart. And The Woman is a sunkenness that She wishes could sizzle and pop and explode like the food on the pan and what song what song what song could a body be in motion and if She could get it and get to it and get out of it and be a thing bigger than this space hovering and tethered.

The Woman on the floor says, I think I have to let go . . .

She says nothing and cares little of The Woman's words and imagines there is a body in motion on a mountain or in the ocean or in very air and aren't they close to being a body in motion in very galaxy and on planets and in solar systems and hushing about the cosmos as wisps and whispers and hums and oh that ache of the stars and forgottenly-damned words made stars and She dreams of being let go—of being—of being let go and coal-hotting to the very wave of the beings around her and then She could be a blood stream or a cellular friction or a slip from air to cloud to rain to Earth and back again and this all in motion to follow the heart-beat-action and this a way of being untethered and unnamed and free and—and all—and all.

. . . but I can't, The Woman on the floor says and picks herself up and steadies her body and her tools and foods and steadies her life and thinks not-yet not-yet not-yet and wakes to her woes and her deep empty and this The Woman knows and feels safe in.

And She is the ch-ch-ch and ghh-ghh-ghh of herself being dragged down the hallway and back to the screens and The Woman closes the video and gets to her voice on form-platted center and too full of self for She to watch. "I had a strange moment today" The Woman begins to type and She feels the letters and the place of The Woman's voice a betrayal and a selfing rude and stubborn and remembers there is such a thing as a cold-heat as there is such a thing as a warm-heat. And wasn't She this cold cold empty thing now trapped. Cramped trapped and dragged. And isn't the cold-heat always in the all ways the space of the dead stuck stuck stuck and orbiting and tethered in the lives of the living until pulled to the mouth again. This once-name, a spiked harrow with teeth.

ACKNOWLEDGMENTS

(in order of publication)

"With Teeth." *Western Humanities Review*, 64.1. Winter 2010.

"The Last Supper." *Last Night on Earth* (anthology). SSWA Press. Fall 2012. P. 91-100.

"Into A Better-Than-Nothing." *Black Candies*. Nov. 2012. (Formerly titled "Tomorrow's Tomorrow").

"A Survivor's Guide." *The Doctor T.J. Eckleburg Review*. August 30, 2013.

"In This Dream of Waking, A Weaver." *As/Us*. Issue 3. Feb. 2014.

Forthcoming in *Diné Reader: An Anthology of Navajo Literature*. Eds. Esther Belin, Jeff Berglund, Connie Jacobs, and Anthony Webster. Univ. of Arizona Press.

"Whitebark Woman." *Elsewhere*. Winter 2014.

"Seven Years of Cups." *The Collagist*. Issue 71. June 2015.

"Herpes of the Heart." *The Butter*. June 2015.

"The Killer of Rabbits and Brothers." *States of Terror*. Eds. Matt E. Lewis and Keith McCleary. Vol. 2. Ayahuasca Pub, Oct. 30th, 2015.

"How We Hold the Dead." *The Offing*. 4 May 2017.

"Cannibal." *Split Lip Magazine*. Aug. 2018.

These stories would not be here without the support and beauty and laughter of my friends and families, mentors and mentees, & ghosts and robots. Nor would it exist as such without the way of the world and words, the nature of all creatures, kéyah (the land this land), and the body through which I/we experience life. These are your stories as much as mine. Thank you for sharing them with me.

My deep appreciation to the Many Voices Project contest, Minnesota State University Moorhead, the Dawson Family Endowment, and other contributors to New Rivers Press for making this possible. To Nayt Rundquist and the editorial staff, thank you for your careful attention and the care you gave to these words and this collection.

Special thanks to JP for always and everything. To Jeanne who sees me and with whom I gather a heart. To my twin-soul, Johanna, who has taught me courage and kindness. To Amy and the orbits we share. And to that dude in the airport angry-yelling into his phone "You make up stories like you make up life!" (and to my best friend for repeating it with me always in laughter and love).

And all my love to those readers and writers with teeth. To fellow werewolf and collaborator Ryan Bradford, a friend to our horrors and black candies. To Susan McCarty for all our words, cakes, and safe places—and for reading this collection as editor, oracle, and friend. To Lee Ann Roripaugh, Laura Hamblin, Melanie Rae Thon, and Lance Olsen for believing and making it so. To Steve Hayward for being there and sharing his vision and sense of adventure with me every day and in all the ways. To my students who teach me how to read again and again. And to Zandria Ann Sturgill for hearing "rabbits, teeth, weird, lost endless but mystic" and creating a dream-true of it for the cover.

Lastly and with much love, I've unending gratitude for François Camoin, who touched the lives of so many people as a writer, professor, mentor, friend, and listener. He will always have a place in my heart for his kindness, support, and willingness to follow my words carefully and joyfully. For saying "Natanya, you're going to have to build your own audience. It's not sitting out there waiting for you" and imagining it could be done. For being the first and only person to say: "You could never disappoint me," even when I wanted to walk away from school and writing for good. And for opening up academia when I thought it had no use for someone like me. François knew the type of advocacy it takes to reach past privilege and imagine a different kind of achievement, intelligence, talent, and experience that doesn't land on the page or an application like it can so easily for others. He could have focused on my unruly grammar, my confusion over tenses (and time itself), the void of Western canonical reading and comprehension I had, and he could have seen the unconventional narrative structures that shaped my writing as obstacles. He didn't and it is one thing to believe in and encourage a misguided and non-traditional student, a person of color, a clueless writer with a wonky heart and wonkier sense of the world, but it's another to clear a space for them and say *Build away. Get yours.* Hágoónee, François. Nizhónígo ch'aanidíínaał.

Ahéhee' shik'éí dóó shidine'é. To all my dear ones, thank you.

ABOUT THE AUTHOR

Yá'át'ééh. Shí éí Natanya Ann Pulley yinishyé. Kinyaa'áanii nishłį, bilagáana bashishchinn. Táchii'nii dashicheii adoo bilagáana dashinalí. Ákót'éego diné asdzáán nishłį. Colorado Springs kééhasht'į ndi Provo Utah déé' naashá. Ahéhee'. I write fiction and non-fiction with outbreaks in collage and have published work in numerous journals, including *The Collagist, Drunken Boat, The Offing, McSweeney's, Waxwing,* and *As/Us*. My work has been anthologized in *#NotYourPrincess: Voices of Native American Women, Exquisite Vessel: Shapes of Native Nonfiction, Women Write Resistance,* and more. A former editor of *Quarterly West* and *South Dakota Review,* I am the founding and managing editor of the Colorado College online literary journal, *Hairstreak Butterfly Review*. I'm an assistant professor of English at Colorado College. I identify as a Navajo woman and my clans through my mother are Kinyaa'áanii (the Towering House Clan) and Táchii'nii (Red Running into the Water People Clan).

ABOUT NEW RIVERS PRESS

New Rivers Press emerged from a drafty Massachusetts barn in winter 1968. Intent on publishing work by new and emerging poets, founder C.W. "Bill" Truesdale labored for weeks over an old Chandler & Price letterpress to publish three hundred fifty copies of Margaret Randall's collection *So Many Rooms Has a House but One Roof.* About four hundred titles later, New Rivers is now a nonprofit learning press, based since 2001 at Minnesota State University Moorhead. Charles Baxter, one of the first authors with New Rivers, calls the press "the hidden backbone of the American literary tradition."

As a learning press, New Rivers guides student editors, designers, writers, and filmmakers through the various processes involved in selecting, editing, designing, publishing, and distributing literary books. In working, learning, and interning with New Rivers Press, students gain integral real-world knowledge that they bring with them into the publishing workforce at positions with publishers across the country, or to begin their own small presses and literary magazines.

Please visit our website: newriverspress.com for more information.

MANY VOICES PROJECT AWARD WINNERS

("OP" indicates that the paper copy is out of print; "e-book" indicates that the title is available as an electronic publication.)

#140 *WITH TEETH*, Natanya Ann Pulley (e-book)

#139 *Trace*, Melanie Figg

#138 *House of the Night Watch*, Tara Ballard

#137 *Oranges*, Gary Peter (e-book)

#136 *Deep Calls to Deep*, Jane Medved

#135 *Boy Into Panther and Other Stories*, Margaret Benbow (e-book)

#134 *It Turns Out Like This*, Stephen Coyne (e-book)

#133 *A Beautiful Hell*, Carol Kapaun Ratchenski

#132 *Home Studies*, Julie Gard (e-book)

#131 *Flashcards & The Curse of Ambrosia*, Tracy Robert (e-book)

#130 *Dispensations*, Randolph Thomas (e-book)

#129 *Invasives*, Brandon Krieg

#128 *Whitney*, Joe Stracci (e-book)

#127 *Rare Earth*, Bradford Tice

#126 *The Way of All Flux*, Sharon Suzuki-Martinez

#125 *It Takes You Over*, Nick Healy (e-book)

#124 *The Muse of Ocean Parkway and Other Stories*, Jacob Lampart (e-book)